Complete Creation by Andy Riedlinger

Edited by Patty Schaff

Original Black & White Edition 2024

www.identityofoliver.com

Andy Riedlinger
About the Author

Andy Riedlinger was born and raised in Williston, North Dakota, and has many fond memories of growing up in his hometown. He still has several good friends living in western North Dakota and often returns to see them. This rural atmosphere provided plenty of inspiration for Hometown Chronicles, the first novel in the Identity of Oliver Series.

Andy has wonderful parents, whose mother worked as a school teacher and whose father worked as a manager in a bustling oil patch called the Bakken. After raising their family, they moved to a retirement community in Ft Myers, Florida, which they absolutely love. He also has two younger sisters, who are each enjoying great careers and family life. One of his younger sisters, who now lives in Tennessee, has four wonderful children and a loving husband who has blessed their family with a thriving chiropractic business. His youngest sister became a pharmaceutical doctor and is raising one delightful child with her charismatic husband, with whom Andy enjoys fishing with when visiting North Dakota.

Andy moved to Fort Collins, Colorado, immediately after graduating high school in 1997 to pursue new adventures and his love for the mountains. In 2001, he graduated from college with a degree in video production and has since become a respected video systems engineer for many of the largest productions in Colorado. He is also a successful entrepreneur who has pursued many business interests in the city of Denver, where he currently lives. He has owned businesses in Colorado's marijuana industry, real estate market, audiovisual industry, as well as two laundromats and a small vending business.

Andy enjoys fishing, hunting, snowboarding, snowmobiling, billiards, oil painting, writing, and traveling in his free time. He began writing at a young age and has continued to chase his dream of being a successful author. Remarkably, he had written some short stories, several poems, and a novella before even graduating high school. He published his first novel in 2007 and has written a number of unique pieces of literature, including five novels, two novellas, short stories, an autobiography, and over one hundred poems.

The Identity of Oliver Series

Author

Andy Riedlinger

The Identity of Oliver Series

Hometown Chronicles is the first book in The Identity of Oliver Series. This remarkable story will introduce you to a handful of exciting characters and their unique relationship with Oliver. Each one of these characters has its own tantalizing story to tell and unique influence over the anomalies Oliver faces. This book explains an incredible love interest and friendships whose futures hang in the balance of small-town injustice. Hometown Chronicles is a philosophical think piece with an intense narrative of true love, unique integrity, and a goal for revenge served ice cold. Be prepared to experience a whirlwind of emotions as this amazing tale of bizarre fate is told. This story will be sure to make you laugh and cry as you read what causes Oliver to embark on extraordinary journeys around the world.

West Coast Chronicles is the second book in The Identity of Oliver Series. This story follows the twisted fate of a young man fleeing from corrupt law enforcement. Oliver takes you up and down America's West Coast on an exuberant adventure in search of his evil nemesis and hippy friend to help save the life of the father to his love interest. However, this isn't a story that only explains physical exploration. It will also lead you on a quest to understand some of life's most intriguing questions and difficult problems to solve. The unique subplots of this book are guaranteed to leave you rolling on the floor with laughter, wiping away tears of sadness, and pondering over the many complex issues Oliver faces. Interactions with punk rockers, ravers, and hippies explain their unique subculture dancing in the lives of ordinary people. West Coast Chronicles will leave you with an intense cliffhanger with its philosophies standing on first, second, and third base. Finally, the Identity of Oliver pitches the next book in the series, which is guaranteed to be a grand slam hit.

Chronicles of Heart and Revenge is the third book in The Identity of Oliver Series. The glitches in Oliver's profound journey through life have finally been exposed. Now all the fantastic pieces of this obscure puzzle come together to form one final enigma to solve. Oliver plans to marry his beloved, but impossible goals must be achieved before the father of the bride walks her down the aisle. These obscure tasks provided a fantastic opportunity to develop the most gripping storylines of the entire series. This leads you to embark on a sequence of anomalous adventures around the globe as Oliver is forced into the seedy underworld of black-market crimes. Prepare yourself to venture into the inner-city slums of some of the world's most dangerous places, as well as tropical islands and beautiful beaches at some of the most exotic destinations on earth. You'll travel to the Philippines, Mexico, Columbia, Switzerland, Denmark, Brazil, the Czech Republic, Costa Rica, Thailand, Nicaragua, Germany, Indonesia, Guatemala, Honduras... fourteen countries in all before Oliver finally meets his nemesis for the last time.

HomeTOWN

ChronicleS

Chapter I

My name is Oliver. I am the oldest of three kids who grew up on a vast 2900-acre farm and cattle ranch in western Nebraska until the winter of 1995. During the first twelve years of my life, my family was responsible for buying, raising, and selling a herd of about five hundred cows each year. I felt content as a young child. I could go as far as to say that if cow shit never existed, I would have had nothing to complain about until the first day I attended public school. My family and I became immune to the horrible smell from our cattle ranch, so I could never distinguish between the stench of fresh cow pie and clean air until several years after I left the ranch. I was in high school before I even knew what cow shit smelled like. Needless to say, I was an outcast amongst my peers throughout the first several years of school.

Down the road from our farmhouse was an average-sized 1100-acre ranch that had been abandoned for as long as I could remember. I had never seen anyone even visiting this ranch until I was about eight years old, and then suddenly, people moved into the house, and cows were in their fields. I think my mom liked the idea of having neighbors because one day, we all dressed up and went to their house with a pie my mom had baked.

The family that had moved in had a teenage son and a daughter the same age as me. This was the day that I met Erica. I thought she was the most beautiful girl I had ever seen before, and as luck would have it, I could see her quite often after our neighborly introduction. This was mainly because of a carpool partnership that was worked out between our two families to transport Erica, her brother, my two sisters, and me to Ogallala, which was the closest town with a school system.

Erica and I became best friends that winter and spent almost every day together after this incredible bond was created. During this time, we discovered that we had many things in common. We were the same age and size, and we both hated cows more than anything else in the world. Three more wonderful years passed, and I remember most of those days being filled with happiness while hanging out with Erica.

We sat beside each other in school and held hands in the hallway. We also spent a lot of time wandering through sunflower and wheat fields playing hide and seek. Erica's family owned about a dozen pigs that we would visit frequently, and my family had a dog that followed us around everywhere we went. My family also owned five horses while I was growing up. One of these horses was given to me on my tenth birthday. I named this horse Baya. Erica and I rode this horse around our farm and ranch at least a few times each week. These experiences were the best memories I had as a child.

Unfortunately, when I was twelve years old, our lives were hit with a strange wave of misfortune when a terrible cow disease began killing off our cows. I remember getting up one morning to put water in the troughs as usual, but there was something wrong about this particular day. Usually, my dad would be yelling, "Get your ass out of bed... time for chores." Then, I would hear the front door slam as he began using all sorts of profanity. However, this morning was different because my dad didn't say much. I eventually went outside and saw my dad looking at a cow lying in the pasture. When I approached him to ask what was wrong, he replied, "I'm trying to figure out wonder what the fuck happened to this cow?"

"What do you mean?" I asked. "Is it not supposed to be sleeping or something?"

"It's not sleeping, Oliver, it's fucking dead! Great! That is all I need is for my goddamned cows to start dying... son of bitch!"

Several more days passed before another cow died, but the day following the death of the second cow, another died, and then another the day after that. As more cows began to die, it led to very drastic and often violent mood swings for my father. He seemed to start a lot of quarrels with my mother during this time, and it only got worse as time went on. It reached a point where my dad appeared to be engaged in a never-ending argument with my mom and anyone who came near him. He would never get physically violent with anyone, but he constantly punched and kicked inanimate objects. Since my dad was a large, beastly man, this appeared very threatening to those around him.

My dad's life was hard all of the time, and I figured that was why he initially developed an alcohol use disorder. After our cows began to die, he started drinking so much that I realized the life he once had was like a redneck paradise in comparison to the problems he presently faced. Watching him get drunk almost every day throughout my early childhood was the most challenging part of my life to understand or deal with emotionally.

I remember one morning when everything seemed to be at its very worst for our family. I had just finished getting ready for school when I came down the stairs and saw my dad standing in the middle of the kitchen, wearing only his underwear. While holding a beer in one hand and disaster in the other, I heard him start yelling at my mom, "If these piles of shit, bastard cows don't quit dying, this whole fucking year is going to hell, and we are going with it!"

My mom often ignored him when he started yelling and usually said things like she did that morning, "If you don't quit swearing like that, I'm not going to listen to you anymore."

I heard my father answer, "It wouldn't make any difference anyway because you don't hear a damned thing I say even if you are listening. Look out at the pasture... you deaf bitch! Those damned cows aren't sleeping... they're fucking dead!"

This poor choice of words my father spoke resulted in one of the shortest fights my parents ever had as my mom turned around with a hot pan filled with my father's breakfast and yelled, "What did you call me?" My dad just stood there shaking his head with a stupid look on his face at this point. Then I heard my mother yell at my father, "Do I look like a cow to you?" Before she even finished her sentence, my dad was lying on the kitchen floor, knocked out with eggs all over his face from the blunt force trauma of a cast iron frying pan. "There's your fucking breakfast, you big, dumb bastard!" This was the first time in my life that I ever heard my mom use the "F" word, and this was the last time in my life that I ever heard my dad say anything mean to my mother.

The next day was very strange because there wasn't a cloud in the sky, but our farm and ranch still seemed covered with clouds. My father had found six more cows lying dead in our pasture that morning, and only a month later, every cow that our family owned had died. After this, things would change dramatically for our family, and we began to hopelessly pack up our belongings in preparation to move.

During this time, my father never drank a drop of alcohol and seemed to quietly follow my mother's instructions as we prepared to move our family into town. I remember this also being around the time my father started occasionally attending AA meetings. I believe this support, my mother's love, and his determination are what finally put an end to his drinking. I'm not sure if he stopped drinking before we started packing or after everything was packed, but either way, I haven't seen him touch a drop of alcohol since I was twelve years old.

Unfortunately, Erica's family was suffering from the same misfortune with their cattle, so they were all packing up their things during this time as well. My family planned to move to Ogallala, and Erica's family planned to move somewhere closer to her grandparents' house in Kansas. The fact that our families would not be living close to each other was more devastating to me than moving away from the only home I had ever known. As time slowly crept closer to the day our family would finally move, it became increasingly difficult for me to accept.

The barn was eventually stripped of everything that could be sold, and the pasture had become just an empty field where millions of cow pies had fallen from the asshole of cattle ranching. It wasn't long before every possession that my family owned and all my childhood memories were packed into boxes. The sadness I felt while wandering around these places echoed through empty space and dust before eventually becoming just a sad memory.

Unfortunately, my sisters and I had to somehow accept this as a part of growing up, and nothing was more devastating than the day that Erica's family finally moved away. The incredible friendship Erica and I embraced was abridged by a gloomy Sunday morning with little time to say goodbye. I could barely fall asleep the night before she left. With only about an hour of sleep, I woke up wanting to see Erica before the sun even began to rise.

When I walked over to Erica's house, it was freezing cold and raining, and the soft glow of an anticipated sunrise barely hit the horizon. I tried my best to avoid the many puddles of mud that seemed to be everywhere I stepped, but I quickly realized that they were pretty much unavoidable, so I was completely soaked by the time I made it to her house. I probably rang her doorbell fifty times before Erica's mom finally came to answer the door.

"Oliver, what are you doing here so early?"

"I wanted to say goodbye to Erica before you all left," I replied.

"That's fine with me, but Erica isn't up yet. It's six o'clock in the morning. We probably won't leave until noon, so why don't you return in a few hours?"

"I guess it is a little early," I responded.

"Okay, we will see you later, Oliver."

"Bye."

Again, I headed back home through the rain and puddles, freezing my little ass off. As I crawled through the barbed wire fence crossing into our ranch, I saw my mother pull away in the truck. She was probably going to church to pray for a new family because no one wanted to go with her for the past several Sundays. A couple of times, she went alone, and I knew that really upset her. It probably didn't help that my dad was in his underwear, staring out the window at our sixteen remaining cows. When I walked back inside the house, I heard my dad put together the longest string of cuss words I had ever heard.

A short while later, I wandered back through the rain, puddles, and barbed wire fence to Erica's house. Finally, the moment arrived when I stood face-to-face with Erica. "Do you think we will ever see each other again?" I asked.

"I sure hope so," she answered. "You are the best friend that I have ever had. I'm sure we will at least keep in touch by letters, and we could probably call each other once in a while."

"Yeah, maybe... but I doubt my dad will let me make long-distance calls."

"Do you know when you are moving?" Erica asked.

"I don't know... maybe tomorrow?" I responded. "I can't tell with my family, but with you gone, there isn't anything I would want to stay here for anyway."

Erica and I continued to walk around for a while before it began to rain again. As the storm increased in intensity, we ran toward a giant elm tree near Erica's house to seek cover from the rain. To catch our breath, we stopped at the bottom of a hill. In the next few minutes that would pass, both of us realized that this was maybe the last time we would ever see each other.

Completely frustrated and almost crying from anger, I picked up a rock and threw it against the tree, "Why does it have to be this way? Why do we have to leave when it was our fathers that screwed up, not us?" Trying to hide my tears, I picked up another rock that was sharp enough to cut through the bark of this giant elm tree. I then spent several minutes carving out Oliver + Erica, which I circled with a heart.

I couldn't wrap my little twelve-year-old head around this moment in time, nor could I predict the future, which made it impossible to understand the significance of the unique work of art I created that day. Nevertheless, this experience was significant enough for me to remember exactly where this tree was located as I continued through life and important enough to Erica that she would at least remember that the carving existed. We didn't know it yet, but these distinctive memories would respectfully embrace our unique romance for many years into the future.

"I will miss you, Oliver!" Erica said, as she looked into my eyes.

"I love you," I said, looking back into her eyes. These words came out of my mouth like unexpected vomit, without even knowing what love was, but they were true... true as any words that have ever been spoken.

"I love you too," she said without hesitation. We stood only a couple of inches apart from one another as these bittersweet words rolled off her tongue. Without even thinking about our actions or understanding the element of romance, we kissed each other for the first time and, perhaps, the last time. The integrity of this moment was so pure and beautiful that it became the prominent memory of my childhood. What I saw when I looked into her eyes that day cannot be recalled or forgotten. It was as if time was lost within a dream and placed in a heart-shaped box that I was only allowed to open once before it disappeared forever.

Following this kiss, Erica looked at me with provocative, beautiful young eyes and said, "I will show you mine if you show me yours."

All choked up and bewildered, I was still just a boy when I said, "Okay."

I saw nothing in the few seconds that our pants were at our knees, which left me completely bewildered at the tender age of twelve. We were just children attempting to understand this experience while standing on the edge of an unpredictable future and holding on to our past for all it was worth. We were not adults yet, but we eventually would be, and this memory followed me around until I got there.

"Goodbye, Erica."

"Goodbye, Oliver, I will miss you."

"Me too," I cried. "Me too..."

Chapter II

It took a while to sell the ranch and the accompanying farm equipment that our family owned, but the day finally came when it was all sold for next to nothing compared to its worth as a healthy cattle ranch. Fortunately, the money was enough to purchase a modest four-bedroom house in town and pay off all of the outstanding bank loans that my family had acquired over the years.

I also believe there may have been roughly ten grand or so left to put in the bank after all the transactions were finalized. Incidentally, my father decided to give this money to my mother to do whatever she pleased after he secured a job at a tractor supply store. I had never seen such generosity in my father's decisions, nor did I see my mother with any more money than what was needed to buy groceries. My mother had three primary responsibilities while our family was living at our house in the country. These were to be a mother to her three kids, a wife to my father, and continuously overcome missed opportunities to follow her passions.

Remarkably, this new prospect not only changed my mother's life, but it also changed the lives of everyone in our family for the better. Ogallala wasn't traditionally a great place for commerce beyond farming, ranching, and essential household items, to the point that the business district would appear as a ghost town to those who didn't actually live there. However, this didn't stop my mother from pursuing the dream of owning her own business. She was determined to beat the odds by fearlessly signing a two-year lease agreement for a small store on Main Street that had previously been vacant for nearly a decade.

She always had a knack for making crafts and developing this into a profitable hobby. This was the initial cornerstone of her business, and she called her business "The Creative Corner." Unfortunately, the sales from her craft items didn't amount to much, but this didn't seem to bother my mother. I remember my dad asking her how sales were going about six months after she opened her store, and she sadly explained that her sales were significantly less than anticipated. Concerned about our family's finances, my dad asked what she planned to do about her failing business model and then indicated that she may have made a mistake opening her store. My mother's response to this was powerful and showed how much confidence she had in herself, "The Creative Corner isn't generating a lot of money right now, but this doesn't mean the business is failing. I'm learning how to create a successful business, Jim, and there is no one that will stand in the way of this. It will take a little time, but my dreams will come true."

I'm nearly certain that the seed money for my mother's business was all my family had in savings, so this was undoubtedly causing some serious financial worries for our family. Nevertheless, my dad didn't continue to inquire into my mother's business after she adamantly expressed her conviction to succeed, but his silent concerns continued for several months.

A few weeks before Christmas, I vividly remember listening to my folks having a conversation while I was hiding behind the corner.

My mother told my dad that business had started to pick up and that The Creative Corner just crushed its single-day sales record on Black Friday. I heard my dad respond with a tone of skepticism, "Wonderful! How much money did you make? I'm sure it had to have been over a hundred dollars."

"You are right about that, Jim. It was definitely over a hundred dollars," my mother replied, seeming to be mildly upset that my father's expectations were so low.

"So, how much money did you make?" my dad asked with a little more enthusiasm.

"I made $2630 in sales and another $420 from service contract commissions."

"What?" my dad replied in a loud, commanding voice. "This is not something to joke around about. Everyone in our family needs new clothes, and I want to know if we can afford to put presents under the tree this year!" This was my main concern at the time as well.

"I'm not joking around, Jim. My gross total sales on Black Friday were just over three thousand dollars!"

"What the hell are you selling... cocaine?"

"No, Jim, I'm not selling drugs for God's sake."

"Then what are you selling?" my dad asked, with continued apprehension in his voice.

"I don't know if you noticed, but that giant phone tower out west of town was finished a few months back. This means Ogallala now has cell phone service, and guess who owns the only cell phone store in western Nebraska?"

"I don't know," my dad responded. "AT&T?"

"No, you shithead, I turned that back half of Creative Corner into a cell phone store, and Black Friday happened to be the grand opening."

"You are joking, right?"

"I am not joking, Jim," my mom replied. "Not only did my store clear over three thousand dollars in sales on Black Friday, but it has cleared almost seven thousand dollars since... and this is only because I ran out of phones to sell to customers. Fortunately, I should get another shipment in by the end of this week." This ended my family's financial hardship, but it was a security that didn't come easy moving forward. This business created problems as well.

Cell phone design and manufacturing were rudimentary at best back in 1997. The cell phones themselves were large and heavy, making them exceedingly difficult to carry around. As impractical as it was to carry this item, it was not at the top of the list of frustrations for your average cell phone owner. Batteries could only provide power to the cell phone for about six hours so long as you were not talking on it, and this time diminished to less than an hour if you were.

Conversely, neither of these two problems even came close to the nightmare you'd experience with cell phone service, particularly in rural Nebraska. You didn't have cell phone companies like Verizon Wireless, T-Mobile, or AT&T to compete for your service like you do now. The cell phone companies that were available at the time were called MCI, WorldCom, Alltel, and Omnipoint. These companies were not concerned about delivering quality service because nobody had anything to compare their shitty service to.

Nowadays, you have service maps, competitive pricing, and reviews to compare the quality of customer service that cell phone companies have to offer. Back then, there was typically only one company that provided monopolized service to massive regions of land. This was because it didn't make sense for cell phone companies to compete if they could create a monopoly where cell service didn't exist.

Ogallala is a perfect example to explain all of this. Alltel built the very first cell tower in western Nebraska, only two miles west of Ogallala. Alltel also built the second tower near Scottsbluff. The third tower was built right on the Nebraska border three miles north of Julesburg, and as you probably could have guessed, this cell tower was subsequently built by Alltel as well.

What this amounted to was that if you wanted your cell phone to work properly in western Nebraska, you needed to buy an Alltel phone and sign an Alltel service contract. This is how Alltel monopolized the cell phone industry in western Nebraska in the late 90s. Incidentally, horrific cell phone design and service limited the cell phone business in Ogallala to only one cell phone store from late 1997 until 2001, which my mother owned. Despite this peculiar monopoly, business slowed down dramatically over the next few months following The Creative Corner's blockbuster sales record set on Black Friday, 1997. Nevertheless, it remained steady enough to provide more than enough income for our family to live very comfortably moving forward... at least in terms of finances.

With this said, the stress brought on by this business was substantial at times, particularly during the first six months. This stress finally reached fever pitch when a very disgruntled customer came into my mom's store and began to yell at her about his cell phone service. My mom tried to calm him down, but everything she said seemed to upset this man even worse until he became completely unglued. He ended up throwing several of my mother's crafts onto the floor, which caused several of these items to break. Then, he threw his cell phone at my mother's face before walking out of the store, and this resulted in a blackeye.

After this angry man left The Creative Corner, my mom called my dad, crying while explaining what had happened. She identified this man as a farmer acquainted with my father, who was known to exercise his drinking problems at some local bars in Ogallala. After coming to my mom's store to comfort her, my dad searched for this man and found him at one of these bars at the north end of town.

I'm not sure how many fights my dad has gotten into throughout his life, but as far as I know, this is the only fight he has been in since I was born. My father was a large, beastly man who stood 6-foot-9 inches tall and weighed nearly three hundred pounds, which usually brought people to their senses real quick when contemplating a fight with him. The fact that my father was a huge man wasn't the only thing that made him scary. His face turned beet red when he got angry, and his facial expression resembled a threatened grizzly bear. With this said, you would not want to be the man who threw his cell phone at my mother and gave her a black eye.

I wasn't there when this fight occurred, but I've been told this story hundreds of times because my dad became somewhat of a local legend after this. The fight happened in Ogallala's busiest bar during its beer and a shot for $1 happy hour, so the place was packed. When my dad found this man, he lifted him up by his neck and smashed his head through the ceiling. Then, he tossed his face into the floor like a football player spiking the ball in the endzone. That is when my dad grabbed his feet and started to vigorously swing this man around in a circle. When he finally let him go, the man flew twenty feet or more across the room and went through a dividing wall separating the pool tables from the rest of the bar. Next, my dad straddled one of his legs backward over his knee and then pushed down on his calf and hamstring until his leg retrograded with a ninety-degree bend in the wrong direction. Once the fight was over, he handed the bartender his credit card to pay for the damages and promptly walked out the front door of the tavern. Legend has it that this man wasn't able to walk, talk, or see clearly ever again and has spent the rest of his life in a wheelchair, eating his food through a straw.

It wasn't typical for the police to respond to a physical dispute in Ogallala, but the sheer brutality of this fight and the damage caused to the bar resulted in every available emergency worker in town showing up at the scene. Incidentally, it took four minutes from the time the fight started until the first police officer arrived, and by this time, the altercation had been over for at least three minutes, so my dad was already long gone. After seeing what my father had done to this man, there wasn't a single person in that bar who dared to provide a witness statement.

This was an extremely fortunate situation for my father because without a witness, there wasn't enough evidence to substantiate probable cause for a violent assault to have occurred, so no investigation ensued. Despite there not being any lawful witnesses to this fight, plenty of actual witnesses definitely told all of their friends and family about it. It didn't take long for everyone in town to become very aware of what not to do if you were unhappy with Alltel's cell phone service. From this point forward, no one living in or around Ogallala during the summer of 1997 has even raised their voice in The Creative Corner.

By January 1998, my mother's business was bringing in enough revenue to hire a full-time employee, giving my mom a lot more time to work on her crafts and do the things she enjoyed. I was now at the legal age to work part-time as well, so I helped out here and there stocking shelves and cleaning the floors to put some spending money in my pockets. This was mostly spent on fishing poles, lures, and hunting equipment until I got my driving license that summer. Then, I focused on saving enough money to buy a 1989 model Honda Civic, which I attained just before starting my sophomore year in high school.

Inspired by my mother's success, my dad started thinking about some things he was good at and eventually went into business for himself as well. His business plan consisted of buying a big-rig semi-truck, which he used to haul all sorts of farm equipment, hay-bales, and grain around the state in the fall. Once the harvest season ended, I didn't see him much for the next six months because he started to travel across the country, hauling all sorts of random shit to random places. It was interesting to picture my redneck dad cruising into New York City in a big-rig semi-truck while talking on his CB radio as he shifted into eighteen-wheel drive and gave'er hell.

When he got bored, he would probably pull over at a truck stop to buy a porno magazine, yell at some teenagers, and refill his 96oz mug full of coffee. If there happened to be a diner connected to the truck stop, he would probably get himself a country-fried steak, a couple of burgers, and a hot dog to go. This is how my dad rolled. He lived his life like he wanted to and didn't care about what anyone thought about him.

During the years our family lived in the country at our farm and ranch, my dad didn't seem to understand the world, and the world didn't seem to understand him. However, his new endeavor with this big-rig semi-truck seemed to provide retribution for many of his misunderstandings with the world.

My dad was drunk most of the time while our family lived on the ranch, so I didn't know what to think of him as a child, but his big-rig semi-truck business made him feel good about himself, and this made me proud to be his son. Around this time, I began to really admire and respect my father's journey through life. This developing admiration caused me to want to spend more time with him. Ironically, the first time in my life that I ever wanted to spend more time with my father happened to be when he was gone the most.

When he returned in the spring, I asked him to go walleye fishing with me a lot more on the North Platte River and at Lake McConaughy. In the summer, I asked him to teach me how to drive his big-rig semi-truck, mostly to spend more time with him, which was reciprocated with conversations and life lessons that strengthened our bond. When fall came around, we spent a lot of time together pheasant hunting at my dad's secret stash spots south of Ogallala with our family dog, a well-trained English Springer Spaniel named Daisy. I experienced the best pheasant hunting of my life that year with my dad, and I will never forget how fun it was chasing birds around with him.

In late November, my dad took off driving around the country again, but this was the last winter he spent away from our family. He returned to Ogallala the following spring with enough money to buy another big-rig semi-truck, so now he had two. This somehow allowed him to stay home most of the time, aside from the months of harvest. I don't completely understand how his business operated the rest of the time, but he just sat around the house talking crazy trucker talk on a long-range CB radio to a couple of guys, "Breaker, breaker, copy, copy, this is Big Jim Billy Bob, what's your twenty, Red Truck One?"

"I'm headed west on northbound highway 604... over."

"Roger that, good buddy. Watch out for Smokeys because there's a couple of Bear Rolling Discos out in that direction... over."

"Copy, copy, Roger that... I'll be pulling into the Chicken Coop here in just a few minutes... over."

"Copy, copy, over and out."

Chapter III

I turned seventeen during the summer between my sophomore and junior year in high school. I started boxing and karate a
year earlier but didn't get good at it until this summer. In addition to
learning how to fight, I spent most of my time fishing and hanging
out in the bowling alley playing pool. By the end of the summer,
I had gotten good at playing pool and started to play in a weekly
eight-ball tournament during the last couple of weeks before school
started. These matches took place at the bar in the bowling alley, and
since I was not yet of legal drinking age, these tournaments were the
only time I could play at these tables.

Almost everyone who played in these tournaments was an older
adult, and the only reason I was able to play with them was that there
were not many people able to compete with the regulars who showed
up each week. There was only one other player in these tournaments
who looked as young as I did, and his name was Billy. I met Billy
for the first time very briefly during the second round in my first
tournament when we were matched to play against each other. He
ended up beating me by only one shot on the eightball, putting him
in the winner's bracket and me in the loser's bracket.

This game seemed to be placed in our lives with an element of
fate because our scheduled games lined up for the rest of the night,

and more importantly, the times when we were not playing games also matched up. By coincidence, we were also parked with our front bumpers facing each other in the parking lot, and we both made it a point to smoke weed between games for good luck.

We awkwardly tried to hide from each other while inconspicuously attempting to get high during the first lull in play, but both of our efforts to keep our cannabis habit a secret failed at the exact same time. I happened to lean over under my dash to take a hit just as he came up from under his dash after taking a hit, and this sequence continued for a couple more tokes until we suddenly found ourselves looking at each other while blowing smoke out our mouths. Then we both started to cough, with smoke rolling out of our windows.

At that moment, Billy and I realized that we were both smoking weed. At first, this low-key epiphany just caused us to stare at each other for about ten seconds feeling paranoid. Then, we both smiled and began to laugh at the situation. This is when we got out of our vehicles and introduced ourselves. We immediately hit it off and acted like close buddies with a long history behind us by the night's end. This would be the start of what would become an incredible friendship.

Billy and I discovered several coincidences and interesting commonalities in our lives over the next few months. We initially discovered we had something more in common besides being potheads and good pool players during a conversation about walleye fishing. Billy told me he owned a 21-foot Lund fishing boat, perfect for fishing the big waves that rolled across Lake McConaughy. He also told me that he didn't have any close friends to fish with, which I also identified with because my only fishing buddies were my dad and a couple of uncles.

Billy and I decided to go fishing at this lake the next time we hung out. I told Billy the night before we went out that I could meet him at his house, but he insisted that he wanted to pick me up. The following morning, we stopped by the bait shop to pick up some night crawlers and a few plugs to pull around the lake. I was surprised to see Billy also buying a twelve-pack of beer to put in the cooler because I had figured he was underage. I knew he was older than me, but I didn't realize how much older he was. It turns out he had just turned twenty-one a few days before we met.

That day on the water was pretty slow, but we did manage to pull out two good-sized walleyes in the morning and a nice six-pound walleye in the afternoon before heading back to the dock. We went fishing a few more times before the lake froze over that year, and each time, Billy insisted that he pick me up from my parents' house. I asked him a couple of other times at the weekly pool tournament if I could come over to his house to smoke a joint and to see where he lived, but he always redirected my inquiries into a conversation, which led away from these questions.

During our last outing for the year at Lake McConaughy, he finally told me that he lived about twenty miles south of Ogallala, another interesting coincidence and commonality we shared. As described more about the place where he lived, it sounded like it was near the farm and ranch where I grew up as a child. This was when I asked him if he had been seeing any pheasants out where he lived, and this exchange unveiled our shared passion for pheasant hunting.

Our discussion started to twist and turn until it eventually resulted in one of the most bizarre conversations I had ever had in my life. It began with Billy explaining how he learned to hunt pheasants. Almost every hunter gets into the sport by learning from their father. There are slight variations to this that may include a different family member or close friend, but 99% of hunters learn how to hunt the same way.

The reason why I initially found Billy's story to be so unique is that he never knew who his dad was while growing up, but he somehow ended up as the sole heir to his father's farm when he passed away in 1995. He moved to this farm in Nebraska in 1996 after turning eighteen. A short time later, he started to notice a bunch of colorful birds on his farm, but he didn't know what they were called. Hunters began knocking on his door as fall rolled around, asking him if they could hunt the pheasants they saw in the harvested corn field on the north end of his farm.

This is when he started connecting the dots because the same cornfield where everyone wanted to hunt was where he saw all these colorful birds. Interestingly enough, one of the hunters he allowed to hunt on his land was very grateful and returned the next day with three small bags full of pheasant breasts for him to eat. Since this meat resembled chicken, he made pheasant fajitas one night. Then he made fettuccine alfredo with pheasant onions, broccoli, and mushrooms the next night. Finally, he fried up some pheasant nuggets on the third night and dipped them in various sauces he picked up from the grocery. He said that after this, he became hooked and determined to figure out how to hunt these delicious birds.

So, he went to the gun store in Ogallala to ask how to get started, and they set him up with a bunch of hunting clothing and several boxes of #5 shot Prairie Storm 3-inch Magnum shotgun shells, as well as information for the type of gun he needed to hunt pheasants. After the gunsmith told him he would need a 12-gauge shotgun to hunt these birds, he went home to see if this was one of his inherited guns. It turned out that he inherited six 12-gauge shotguns, so he went out that same afternoon and started chasing pheasants around his farm.

He told me that he spent every day hunting pheasants for the next two months. I found it amusing as hell to listen to how he went about this. He said he initially spent a week running around his cornfields chasing birds but couldn't get close enough to shoot one of them. He even tried using his 4-wheeler to chase the birds, but the results were even worse than chasing them around on foot.

Finally, in the late afternoon on his fourteenth day of pheasant hunting without any luck, he saw a bird looking pretty stupid near some thistle right next to the road about a mile down from his house. This was when he stopped his truck for a moment to strategize. Once his gun was loaded, he floored the gas petal until he got up on the pheasant. He said that he was so excited not to have seen this bird fly away that he jumped out of his truck before he even put it in park. Miraculously, he managed to kill this bird with his first shot. Then, just as he ran out into the field to retrieve it, nine more roosters flew out of that tiny little clump of thistle only about four feet away from him. He said that he took two more shots and killed three more birds.

"Wow," I said, "so, you spent fourteen days hunting pheasants without shooting a single one... then shot a double and bagged your limit in less than a minute?"

"I sure did!" Billy proudly said, with a giant grin on his face.

"Did you ever figure out how to hunt the pheasants in your field?" I asked.

"Fuck no," Billy answered. "I drive by them all of the time, but as soon as I stop my truck and get out of the vehicle, those birds have already run a hundred yards further into the field. I don't really even hunt my land much, to be honest. I usually go further south looking for thistle clumps alongside the road because that is where I'm successful."

"Wait, you're saying that you own a farm in western Nebraska but don't hunt the land?"

"I do when it snows out," Billy explained. "I can bag a limit pretty easily while driving around my farm if it snows more than couple inches. I have pulled several more out of that little patch of thistle where I shot my first pheasant. I also have shot some flying out of a couple of catch basins on the west side of my farm. There is also a sunflower field on the south end of my farm that holds a lot of birds because of a big grassy hill that runs beside it, and there is also an old ranch house down the road from my house that typically holds a flight of birds. I also have a few grain bins with long grass around them that typically hold a bird or two. On the southern corner of my farm, there are fourteen half-mile tree rows that hold a ton of birds, but every time I walk down one side... the birds fly out the other, and since those tree rows are all pine trees, I can't ever get clear shot at them."

"Wait, you have fourteen half-mile tree rows on your farm?" I asked.

"Yeah, some of them are probably not quite a half-mile long, but there are definitely fourteen of them," Billy answered. "I have a couple dozen other tree rows on my farm as well, but I don't know what kind of trees those are. I think they may be hickories or beech trees. I'm not sure. All I know is that they don't hold many birds."

"You have to be kidding me," I responded in disbelief. "How big is your farm?"

"About 4300 acres," Billy replied.

"4300 acres!" I yelled. "You own a 4300-acre farm... holy shit!"

"What... is that big or something?" Billy asked, seeming to have no clue that his farm was over four times the size of an average farm in western Nebraska.

"Yes!" I replied. "That is gigantic!"

"I kind of thought so," Billy said, "but it's hard to compare my farm to others because I don't talk to many people in the area. I lease my land and farm equipment to a couple of farmers who live down south near Binkelman, so I know them. And one of those farmers has a hot daughter who comes to my farm to ride horses with me, so I know her too. I also know you and a few people I've met at the weekly pool tournament, but that's about it.

"So, you just woke up one morning and were told that you suddenly owned a 4300-acre farm right in the middle of God's country?"

"Pretty much," Billy answered.

"Holy shit! That is a goddamned miracle. You have never hunted this land with another person before?"

"No, I've only hunted by myself."

"Have you ever hunted with a dog before?"

"No, it's always just me."

"Dude, listen, we have to change that," I said. "Next Friday is opening day... I will be hunting with my dad on Friday and Saturday, but I can bring my dog to your farm on Sunday. If you don't let anyone hunt your land before then, I can guarantee you an easy limit. I have a well-trained English Springer Spaniel named Daisy. All I have to do is yell, "Circle the field, Daisy," and then toss my hand up for her to run around your cornfield to chase the birds toward us.... and that's only one of six strong commands that we have trained her to execute. She also does a back-and-forth sweep. She can walk down one side of a tree row while you walk down the other, and there is also a command to make her zig zag back and forth between the trees. She also understands a great catch basin command."

"That sounds awesome!" Billy replied. "I just don't know if I want to hunt at my farm."

"Why in the hell not?" I asked, dumbfounded.

"Okay, so here is the thing, Oliver. There is an acre of land somewhere on my farm where I grow weed, so I get nervous showing people where my farm is," Billy said hesitantly. "I have spent most of my life locked up, and I don't want to go back to that."

"Then why are you even growing weed?" I asked.

"To sell it."

"So, you grow an acre of weed... which you sell... and you're worried about bringing my dog out to your farm to go pheasant hunting?"

"It sounds nuts... I know," Billy replied.

"Hold on... wait a second. I'm trying to wrap my head around all this," I replied with a head full of questions, "You said that you were locked up for nearly your entire life, and you don't want to go back to that... I don't understand. How were you locked up for so long?"

"I was an orphaned child who was found in a car seat lying in a McDonald's parking lot when I was three months old. Unfortunately, I was supervised by the state in some way or another for fifteen years of my life after that. The first six years of my life were spent in a state transitional facility, waiting for someone to adopt me. Unfortunately, these six years of my life really fucked me up.

I was about three years old when I started understanding emotional connections with other human beings. I learned this because there wasn't anyone who stayed in my life long enough to love me. All the orphaned children I made friends with kept on getting adopted, but for some reason, nobody wanted me. There were also a lot of state employees involved in my early childhood development, but they never worked at the state adoption facility for more than a year. So, not only was I not getting adopted, but everyone I ever knew left me shortly after getting to know them, and I didn't know why. Sadly, by age four, I completely understood that nobody loved me. When I was five years old, I started to ask why nobody loved me, which was also about the time that I started hating the world for not giving me parents or friends. That was the year I started acting bad.

Unfortunately, by the time I was finally adopted at six years old, I wanted to avenge the world. The cruel irony about this was that I spent the first five years of my life acting good, wanting desperately for someone to love me. I am certain that if I had been adopted before I turned five, I would have been able to appreciate love, and I likely would have grown up being a good kid. Unfortunately, I missed this opportunity, and so did my foster parents.

I acted so bad after being adopted that I was caught breaking over a dozen laws in just two years. These crimes started off as petty but quickly escalated into more serious charges. I committed two juvenile felonies and finally burned down my neighbor's house. After this, I spent the next four years of my life in the Nebraska State Mental Institution for Radically Disturbed Children and the following five years in a maximum-security juvenile detention facility."

"Wow!" I replied. "That is some heavy shit, dude... you burnt down a house?"

"Well, not a whole house. It was more like half a house," Billy responded, "and it is not like I went over there with a gas can and lit it on fire. It started because I lit one of their trash cans on fire next to the garage, and that started the garage on fire, which had a lot of flammable liquids in it. The flammable liquids are what started the house on fire. Unfortunately, law enforcement has a challenging time taking this sort of information into consideration when it comes to official charges. Technically, I lit a trash can on fire, and that caused a house to burn down, but the police reports just say I was an arsonist who burned down a house."

"That is an interesting perspective," I replied.

"Yeah, the system is corrupt. If you don't have a good attorney, you are fucked, and if you do have a good attorney... typically, you're still pretty fucked."

"I don't doubt that," I replied.

"Fortunately, when I was seventeen years old, some official-looking state employee came to the detention center where I was being detained to tell me some information that changed my life. She told me that my father had died, and I was to receive his inheritance. Then she went on to explain that my dad never married, had no other kids, and never even made an official will before he died. However, because of some new state law and a glitch in the matrix, the state had to investigate if my father had any kids when he died before acquiring his assets for auction, and by some miracle, the state investigator found me.

This was both bizarre and life-changing information, to say the least, because the state made many attempts to find my parents while I was growing up with no success, but once my father died, it appeared to be relatively easy to find out that I was his son. I guess by this time in my life, there were computer databases to organize hospital records, criminal history, DNA, and other useful investigative tools that were not available when I was a child.

My world changed almost immediately after receiving this information. Up until this life-changing epiphany occurred, I had imagined being a lifelong criminal and assumed that this would eventually lead to a life sentence prison term. I still had about a year left to spend in the correctional facility before I was released, but now I knew that there was something waiting for me when I got out beyond a life of crime.

Over the next several months, while waiting to be discharged, I learned a lot about myself. Most importantly, I figured out that I wasn't a bad person. I just hated the world and acted bad because of it. This information instantly changed my perspective about the world's intentions.

Also, my psychiatrists, therapists, and particularly the juvenile detention officers never gave me incentive for good behavior or to be a moral person. They just explained in one way or another that I was a fucked up kid and the consequences for acting bad would cause my life to get worse. The thing is... my life couldn't get any worse from my perspective. My parents abandoned me in a McDonald's parking lot, for Christ's sake. I had no friends, no one to love, and no one who loved me. I was locked in some room or another for twenty-three hours a day. I was told when to eat, sleep, and shower. The worst part was that I had no privacy at all... I couldn't even take a shit without someone watching me."

"Wow, dude, that must have been horrible," I responded.

"It was horrible," Billy replied. "It was important for me to learn that just because I acted bad for a part of my life, this didn't make me a bad person. Every day since I made this realization, I've tried to act good and be an honest person. I may not be perfect, but I am far from the horrible human being that people described me to be when I was growing up."

"I bet you were one happy person when you were finally released from the correctional facility," I said.

"Oh, you better believe it!" Billy replied. "I was brought into a conference room just before I was released to speak with the state attorney about my inheritance. "This is when I found out that my father was a farmer, or at least appeared to be a farmer. His farming operations were managed by someone else, but in around about way, this made me a farmer moving forward, and with substantial assets to become one.

I was handed a stack of deeds and documented assets at that point. I had deeds to 4300 acres of farmland, a five-bedroom house, a massive detached garage, a giant barn, an old ranch house, a 1994 F-250 extended cab pickup, a 1987 Ford Bronco, a 1957 Chevy Hot Rod, a 1967 Notchback Mustang project car, a 1991 Claas Lexion combine harvester, a 1984 John Deer front load tractor with all sorts of farm equipment trailers, a Harley Davison motorcycle, a Honda CRF dirt bike, a ski-doo snowmobile, two 4-wheelers, and a ton of other miscellaneous items."

"Wow, your farm must be one hell of a lucrative operation," I remarked.

"It is a pretty decent operation, but the money generated from this farm isn't what paid for all this shit. The attorney also explained to me that my father was a meth cook and dealer who blew himself up cooking meth. When they searched the property, they found the largest supply of meth ever recovered by Nebraska law enforcement."

"Holy shit... there is no way this can be true," I said, suddenly understanding a bizarre coincidence.

"I'm not lying. Everything I've told you is true," Billy said, visibly taken back by my response.

"That's not what I am talking about. Is your house at the inter-section of County Road 10 and Basin Road?"

"Ummm... yes it is," Billy answered with a look of surprise. "How did you know?"

"That's the house that I grew up in," I replied. "Your farm used to be my family's farm and ranch, as well as my childhood sweetheart's ranch.

"Really?" Billy asked in disbelief.

"Yes, really."

What I learned that day about Billy's life and the assets he attained would change my life in many ways. Billy became my best friend after this conversation, and I wish that was all I had to write about. Unfortunately, the heartbreaking tale Billy described about the first eighteen years of his life was not where his tragic story ended. What this meant for my future would be profound, to say the least, but for now, it just meant having a wonderful place to hunt pheasants with my new best friend, and I guess it also left me with one hell of a story to tell.

Chapter IV

DURING MY JUNIOR YEAR, I introduced Billy to Adam and Eric, a couple of stoner friends of mine. Once they figured out that Billy was my new best friend, they wanted to hang out with me a lot more because he could provide easy access to booze and weed. This also seemed to attract a handful of girls looking to party on the weekends.

Once I started bringing Billy with me to some of the High School parties and introduced him to some of the girls in my class, I think that he could have had sex as much as he wanted to. However, he wasn't that type of guy and had a strict no-touching policy for high school girls, which demonstrated an impressive level of restraint from the perspective of men. Girls flashed him their tits and flirted with him constantly with no success in their pursuits of seduction, which helped to make him irresistible from the perspective of women.

What was unusual and ironic about Billy was that he constantly seemed to be joking around about women, whether it be talking about fucking some girl or describing how nice of tits one had. However, this was simply shop talk and was always said with a sarcastic tone in his voice. The fact was that Billy was a perfect gentleman for the most part when it came to women. He was always very polite. He opened doors for them and addressed women older than him by saying, "Ma'am," whether they liked it or not, and he always spoke up if he saw another man disrespecting a woman. Plus, I never saw a woman pay for a damn thing when Billy was around either, which explained another reason he was popular with females.

He had every opportunity in the world to be a womanizer. Some country girls would have agreed to have a kid with him simply because he had a farm in the country with horses in the barn. He wasn't a bad-looking dude either, at least not by my standards as a straight guy. He wore a cowboy hat, boots, and wranglers not as a beacon of fashion, but because ranch wear went with his work line. Hell, I even found this to be sexy. There were dozens of times I happened to be sitting next to Billy when high school girls flashed their tits at him simply out of habit, and there were multiple times when I saw a drunk girl walk right up and offer him a blowjob. However, he never reciprocated these drunken propositions by even allowing them to touch him.

With this said, he wasn't made of stone either. If a woman decided that she wanted to whip her tits out in front of him, he would look just like any other man on the planet, but that's mechanical, not disrespectful. As far as know, the only girl who ever had sex with him while I was in high school was with an older woman by at least five or six years.

She was from a super small town called Benkelman, about fifteen minutes south of his farm. She dressed in ranch wear, too, based on occupation, and good God, was she ever sexy... like the sexiest woman that you've ever seen in your whole life, and she was probably even sexier than that. She came to his farm on the weekends to ride horses around, and I just assumed Billy got rode around as well because she was the only person besides myself who was allowed to shoot the pheasants in his tree rows. As hot as that sex must have been, I was never told a damned thing about it, but he had no trouble talking about women like he was a drunken playboy if he didn't plan ever to touch them.

Adam and Eric somehow figured out how to use Billy's popularity with women to their advantage. It was a common occurrence to see them making out with girls at high school keg parties. My friendship with Billy had a unique fringe benefit because I was often sitting beside him smoking weed when girls came by to flash him their tits. However, his moxie didn't lead me to have any make-out sessions with party girls like what Adam and Eric experienced. I just had bad luck and no game to pick up on high school chicks, it seemed.

Eventually, my friends noticed that I never seemed to hook up with anyone and started to make fun of me. I was embarrassed to admit to them that my only sexual experience with a girl occurred during a unique proposition from my childhood sweetheart when I was twelve years old. As horrible and desperate as this may sound, my New Year's resolution that year was to make out with a girl. Incidentally, this peculiar goal of mine materialized just a few weeks into January. This monumental experience occurred at a party when a very forward girl forced my hand up her shirt and began to kiss me right in front of all my best pals.

Thankfully, this was enough action to stop my pals from making fun of me, but it didn't stop my frustrations with women. My interest in the opposite sex and personal curiosity were two important elements of my New Year's Resolution. However, the primary contributing factor was mitigating the embarrassment brought on by my peers.

Unfortunately, there weren't many girls that went to high school with me that I was attracted to, and chalking up random make-out sessions at parties wasn't my top concern like it was for Eric and Adam. The truth was that I was consciously and mindfully searching for an actual girlfriend during my junior year in high school. Unfortunately, the harder I tried to find a girlfriend, the fewer options there seemed to be. I was about to give up entirely until I noticed a girl that I hadn't recognized before. There couldn't have been more than three hundred kids that attended our school, so it was pretty obvious that she was a new student.

This girl was different than the other girls that attended our school. I noticed that she obviously was not concerned with typical clothing trends because she didn't dress like any other girls in our school. I thought it was sexy that her wardrobe blended nicely with her mysterious personality, but what really elevated my sexual attraction was that I thought she was gorgeous and wasn't afraid to show off her legs or cleavage.

She liked wearing black skirts, with black lace or fishnet stockings, and she walked around wearing authentic Vans or Doc Martin boots. She also wore a wide variety of lowcut shirts and several band shirts, which she customized with mindful scissor cuts to ensure that at least a little of her cleavage was showing. Unlike the petite frame of most high school girls, she had a full figure with perfect breasts and a nice round butt. Ironically, these were the only parts of her body that jiggled. She was otherwise a petite woman with small feet, tiny hands, a little nose, and the cutest ears I have ever seen.

I envied everything she would touch and found myself going out of my way to see her between classes. I had to find out who this girl was, but I was far too shy to talk to her. At some point, I knew she had caught on to my admiration. I figured this out because she would sometimes flirt with me from a distance.

I remember that she wasn't wearing a bra one day, which was intentionally advertised in the most seductive way possible. She was wearing a very, very loose, scissor-cut Cure band shirt that showed off her waistline and partially exposed her breasts. Incidentally, she was keeping her skimpy top a secret with a black hooded sweatshirt until the right opportunity came along.

This opportunity occurred during lunch break when she caught me lost in a predictable gaze while standing only twenty feet away. She pulled her hoodie over her head the moment she noticed me looking at her and intentionally pulled up her shirt with it for a few mindful seconds, which exposed her hard, quarter-sized nipples and perfect jiggling breasts. Then she smiled at me after she pulled her shirt back down and noticed me still looking at her, shy and unashamed.

I couldn't look away from this enchanted real-time sexual fantasy, and she obviously didn't expect me to because her well-planned wardrobe malfunction was only partially completed at this point. I stood there wearing track pants with a full erection and had goosebumps, knowing she was just as aroused by this as I was. I watched her bend over while tossing her hair back and grabbing her knees. The scissor cuts in her shirt were purposely cut for this exact moment to occur as she moved her shoulders in a soft, mesmerizing, jigging titty motion while the world clock counted in its head... one

Mississippi... two Mississippi... three Mississippi... four Mississippi... five Mississippi... six Mississippi...

Halfway through the seventh Mississippi, she suddenly began to walk down the hallway straight toward me. She stopped only a couple steps away, which was close enough to smell an intoxicating aroma of female pheromones accented with grape bubblicious gum, cherry red ChapStick, and CK1 perfume. I looked into her eyes with unambiguous intentions to kiss her, and she looked into my eyes with unequivocal intentions to kiss me. Then she gently bit the corner of her lower lip with a seductive expression. My heart was racing as her hungry eyes continued to stare into mine before mindfully becoming fixated on my lips... but I could not bring myself to kiss her. I was paralyzed by unfamiliar desire, untamed teenage emotion, and the inexplicable suggestive nature of this moment. I said nothing... she said nothing... and so nothing happened. We both just walked down the hallway to our next class.

Over the next couple of weeks, I had several more provocative encounters with the mystery woman. However, these experiences were nowhere near as alluring as her titty flash wardroom malfunction. After weeks of curiosity, she finally approached me in the hallway with a tap on my shoulder. When I turned around, I saw the mystery woman looking at me with a big gorgeous smile.

"Hey, Oliver, how are you?

"What?" I replied after several seconds of awkward moments passed.

"How are you doing?

"Fine...I guess."

"Don't you recognize who I am?"

"Ummm…" I had no idea who this was aside from the fact that I was infatuated with her.

"Erica… your childhood best friend."

"Oh my God, Erica!" I excitedly replied. "You look way different than you did five years ago."

"In a good way, I hope," Erica responded.

"Yes, in a perfect way," I replied. "You are absolutely gorgeous!"

"Thank you… that might explain why I catch you staring at me all the time."

"Yeah, that would have something to do with it," I said. "How long have you known who I am?"

"I knew who you were the moment I saw you," Erica replied.

"Then why did it take three weeks for you to talk to me?"

"I thought it was adorable and amusing how you would stare at me with puppy dog eyes all the time… and I guess it just took some time to work up enough nerve actually to say something to you," Erica answered.

"I see."

"Listen, I don't have any tests to take for the rest of the day. Would you maybe want to skip your afternoon classes with me to catch up?"

"Absolutely," I replied with noticeable excitement.

We initially spent about an hour talking in the city park pavilion, but Erica eventually asked if I wanted to go to explore where we used to live. She had not been out that way since moving to Ogallala. I explained to Erica about the incredible coincidence that my best friend now owned the farm and ranch where we used to live and that he was pretty secretive about having people out there.

Nevertheless, after some heavy flirting and clever persuasion, I agreed to go after explaining some boundaries to Erica before leaving. I thought that Billy would likely understand the situation if he were to see us, but I told her that if we saw Billy at any point in time, we would need to leave immediately. Erica understood the assignment as we started driving south into God's country.

Once we arrived at our rural destination, we walked hand in hand toward the fields where we used to ride Baya. After wandering through a sunflower field and around a long bobbed wire fence, we eventually found ourselves on top of a hill. We stopped there to see where we grew up and all our favorite hangout spots from childhood.

When Erica saw her house, she was shocked to see that it had not been taken care of at all. It looked like it may have been vacant ever since she moved away years ago. It was painted with a rather odd color blue the summer after Erica's family moved into the house, but it didn't appear to have much of any color now. There were some other random structures scattered around her old house that were not being used, or rather, couldn't be used. All of these buildings started to deteriorate before Erica's family even moved to the ranch, and now they were in shambles, just waiting to be torn down at this point.

Memories of this place didn't typically haunt me, but that day had a different dynamic. Some memories were fantastic and made me happy. Others were like watching your dog die. There was also an elephant in the room. I was reluctant to tell Erica about the history of the house that claimed the life of the town's most infamous drug dealer, and I certainly didn't want to tell her that Billy grew marijuana on his farm. Living in such a small town, some people really hated potheads. I just wasn't sure how she would react to this story.

Later in the afternoon, we walked over to another field that was just starting to grow corn. This is one of the only fields Erica and I specifically remember as children because an old rusty tractor stopped for the last time right in the middle of it. This tractor was in that field since before I was born. We climbed onto the tractor for a while and pretended we were farmers. That was when we noticed that the corn was being irrigated by pipes that were over one hundred feet long with big wheels attached to them so they could spin around in circles.

"Do you know how these pipes spin around?" Erica asked.

"I have no idea, but it is something that I have often wondered," I replied, pondering the even greater mystery of where the water came from because there wasn't a lake or river around for miles.

After following our childhood footprints around for several hours, these fantastic thoughts and rural mysteries faded into a beautiful horizon with colorful tones of deep purple and burning amber. Just before sunset, Erica and I encountered a magical place full of childhood memories. This was a giant elm tree that we used to climb as kids. It was wonderful to see it growing majestically into the sky and looking as healthy as we remembered. It warmed our hearts when Erica and I saw my carving of a heart around (Oliver + Erica) still carved into this tree.

Erica and I were together pretty much every day following our second introduction. One of the first nights we hung out, I brought her up to a place known as the "Starry Place," a giant grain container that stood on a hill outside town. You could climb up to the top and see the entire city of Ogallala. This was a wonderful place for kids to come and make out or break underage drinking laws.

"Where are you taking me, Oliver?" Erica asked.

"You'll see... it's a surprise."

"Is it someplace fun?"

"Yeah, it will be fun."

Once we arrived at the Starry Place, we climbed up the stairs to the very top of the grain container and looked out toward the twinkling lights of Ogallala. Then we sat down with alluring grins, twisted tongues, and an unpolished enigma of fresh teenage romance.

"Have you ever had a girlfriend?" Erica asked.

"Yeah, I've had a couple of girlfriends, but nothing serious." I was lying because I didn't want her to know about my inexperience with women or how desperate I was to find a girlfriend. "What about you? Have you had any boyfriends?"

"Yeah, I've had a few boyfriends," Erica replied.

"Did you get serious with any of them?"

"Not really," Erica answered with a burning question on the tip of her tongue, "Have you ever had sex before? Because I haven't."

"Really?" I replied. This statement intrigued me as much as it surprised me. Whether or not she ever had a serious boyfriend, I just figured that she had sex at least a few times based on the promiscuous ways she grabbed my attention in the hallways at school.

"Yeah, you act surprised," Erica said.

"Hummm... I just thought.. that..."

"Well, what, Oliver?"

"After what happened in the hallway and everything," I replied, feeling awkward and aware that I just shoved my foot in my mouth.

"I did that just to fuck with you, Oliver," she answered. "I'm not really a slut."

"That is good to know," I said, joking, "Because if you were, I would probably have to take advantage of you."

"Oh yeah... and how would you do that?"

"It's a secret... but if you're lucky, I might bring you on this thrill ride a little later," I said with a smirk on my face, hoping that I didn't sound like an absolute jackass.

"I would love to experience this thrill ride with you," Erica said. "Have you been practicing with a blow-up doll or something?"

"Funny," I replied, searching for something witty to say.

"So.... Oliver, have you ever buried the bone?" Erica asked while scooting a little closer to me.

"What the hell?" I responded.

"Dunked the donut?"

"Huh?"

"Have you ever taken little Oliver for a dive in the deep end?"

"Mmmm..." I muttered while shaking my head back and forth. I figured she was talking about sex, but I didn't want to answer her questions in case I was wrong. I also didn't know how to answer this question and sound cool while doing it.

Finally, with belly roll laughter, she asked, "Have you ever gotten drunk on Mad Dog 20-20 and climbed in the back of a van at the drive-in to fuck a midget in the ass while eating jalapeño?"

I didn't find this as funny as she did, but I laughed along with her even though it felt like she was making fun of me. After an awkward break in conversation, I asked, "Are you asking if I ever had sex?"

"No! I'm talking about fucking a midget in the ass here, man… stay with me," Erica replied. I didn't respond and decided to wait for her to start making sense. Finally, she digressed and said, "What else would I mean? Yeah… have you ever had sex before?"

"Well, once, but it wasn't for very long." I was just flat-out lying my ass off, and I didn't even know why.

"Did you like it?" she asked with a disappointed look.

"I really don't remember. I was pretty drunk…" or dreaming, but what was the difference at this point? Embarrassed and feeling stupid, I knew I had just created a mess that would be hard to clean up.

"Drunk sex, huh? I heard that is the worst kind of sex."

"Yeah, it wasn't that great," I replied. An awkward silence followed this ridiculous lie for almost a minute before I attempted to distract us from the comments I made about my imaginary sexual experiences. "Hey, wasn't that funny… what we did right before you moved away?"

"What thing?" Erica asked.

"The whole… I will show you mine if you show me yours… thing."

"Yeah, actually, that was pretty funny because you had such a small dick back then," Erica answered with a serious and somber tone. I realized her sarcasm when she started laughing again.

"I was twelve. What did you expect to see? You weren't exactly a grown woman yet, either. As a matter of fact, I don't remember seeing anything between your legs," I snapped back, having no idea where this conversation was headed. I just hoped it wasn't going to circle back around to my imaginary sex life.

"Yeah, well, my pussy is just as bald as it was back then," Erica said with clever seduction.

"You have a bald pussy?"

"Yep, I like to keep it nice and slippery."

"It's slippery?" I responded with a look of puzzling seduction.

"Slippery when wet," Erica answered with a flirtatious tone, "but my Bon Jovi wax is really none of your business."

"So, you won't show me yours if I show you mine?"

"What are you trying to say here, Oliver?" she asked, moving closer. We were now sitting shoulder to shoulder. "Do you want to see my pussy?"

"It certainly wouldn't be at the bottom list of things I want to see," I said. Moments later, the purpose of coming to this place was answered with a wet, sloppy kiss. This steamy situation quickly escalated with a burning desire to feel Erica's tits. Unfortunately, my attempt to take her bra off was terrible at best. I had no idea what I was doing. After struggling for a minute or so, Erica just reached behind her back with one hand and unlatched the thing while using her other hand to rub my inner thigh. Once the bra was loose, my hands were free to feel Erica's titties for the first time. When my fingers finally touched Erica's nipples, it seemed as if I had reached the pinnacle of manhood. I felt like an absolute stud, at least for a moment or two.

"Burr... Oliver, your hands are freezing," Erica said, suddenly grabbing my hand out from under her shirt.

As she said this, I thought to myself that maybe I was doing something wrong. Puzzled, I simply responded, "What?"

"Your hand, Oliver... it's freezing cold!"

"I'm sorry. Am I doing something wrong?"

She then grabbed both my hands and said sympathetically, "No, you're doing everything right, Oliver. You just need to tell your hands to warm up. That's all."

"Is it my left hand or my right hand... or is it both my hands?"

"No, it's just this hand," she said, reaching toward me. "Here, let's warm it up." Then she put my hand in between her two hands and rubbed vigorously back and forth while blowing on them. After about twenty seconds, she said, "There, that ought to do it."

"Now what?" I asked.

"Now grab my tits again and see what happens," Erica replied, as she leaned in for another kiss. In the heat of passion, Erica guided my hands all around her body until they were right between her legs, feeling God's greatest creation. It was two o'clock in the morning and well past our curfews by the time we finally decided to get dressed. We didn't realize what time it was because we were too busy kissing, touching, and feeling the moment we fell in love.

Chapter V

"I love you."

"I love you too, Oliver," Erica responded, while we lay in the grass looking up at the sky one summer afternoon. The words "I love you" were often said without even thinking about it as Erica and I sat close to one another. Summertime had drawn us very close. We had spent nearly every day together since school finished for the year. It was now approaching fall, and the sunflowers were in full bloom. Looking out onto endless fields of giant yellow flowers was a very pretty sight. An old, abandoned red barn was built right in the middle of one of these fields. Erica and I would often come to this place to be alone.

"Hey, want to smoke a little weed?" This was the first time I ever asked Erica this question. I loved smoking weed, and I loved Erica, so I thought this question just made sense.

"I don't smoke pot," Erica replied.

"Well, I do."

"Only losers do drugs," she responded with a little bit of sarcasm.

"Come on... everybody is doing it," I said, with my own bit of sarcasm.

"Whatever Oliver."

"Have you ever tried it?" I asked.

"No."

"Do you think you ever will?"

"Maybe," Erica said, after taking a quick moment to think about it.

"Do you want to smoke the joint I have in my pocket?" I asked.

"Not today, Oliver, maybe tomorrow."

"Okay, but a little weed would make today just as awesome as tomorrow." Just as I said this, a fox ran out from behind the barn and into the sunflower field. As I saw this from the corner of my eye, I pointed it out and said to Erica, "Hey, did you see that?"

"What?" she said, turning her head.

"A fox just ran into the sunflower field!"

"Oh, really?"

"Yeah, I guess you missed it."

"I guess so," she said. "I was looking at those two butterflies over there. They are huge, huh?"

"Yeah, they are pretty big, I guess. Do you know what would make looking at those butterflies a hell of a lot more kick-ass?"

"What?" Erica asked, a little annoyed.

"If we smoked the joint I have in my pocket."

"Oh, my God! You're a total pothead, huh?"

"Yes, I am," I said, "and you could be my stoner girlfriend."

"Not today," Erica said. "Maybe tomorrow."

"Give ten good reasons why you shouldn't smoke weed, and I will leave you alone."

"Well, first of all," Erica said, as she began to count on her fingers. "It's not good on your lungs."

"That's bullshit! My lungs feel great!" I responded.

"Second, it makes you stupid."

"If it makes you so stupid, then how come our friend Adam is so smart?"

"This is stupid!" Erica replied. "No matter what I say, you're going make some stupid comment, and eventually, I'm just going to get pissed off!"

"Okay, I'll shut up... please go on."

"Well, third... it's against the law. Fourth, I would get into deep trouble if I ever got caught. Fifth, I probably wouldn't like getting high. Sixth, people act stupid when they are high. Seventh, people sound stupid when they are high. Eighth, ummm.... eighth, people can tell when you smoke it because you smell funny. Ninth, people will call you a pothead if they know you smoke pot, and finally, I just don't want to!"

"That is all you got?" I said while laughing.

"If you come up with ten good reasons why smoking pot is good for you, maybe I will change my mind."

"I'm not saying pot is good for you," I explained. "I'm just saying pot is good, generally speaking."

"Okay, let's hear it," Erica said, while crossing her legs and touching her forehead with a single pointer finger as if she were really preparing to listen.

"Remember study hall last year, when we were in class together right after lunch?"

"Like the only class we actually had together?" she replied.

"Yeah, that one," I replied. "I remember smoking a joint with Adam before coming to class that day. When I got to the study hall, I suddenly really wanted to study math. Unfortunately, I started laughing every time I tried to add more than single-digit numbers together. Finally, I pushed a button on my calculator, and it randomly showed the number 5318008. Then, I spun the calculator around, and it stopped upside down on my desk. When I looked at the calculator again, this number looked as if it said BOOBIES, and then I started laughing so fucking hard that everyone started looking at me."

"That is because you looked like a moron," Erica interrupted.

"No," I replied. "It was because this was the funniest thing I had ever seen a calculator, math, or anything having to do with numbers ever do... and it happened right in the middle of study hall!"

"Did you get the munchies and start hallucinating?" Erica asked.

"No, I think the number six on my calculator actually turned into a cheeseburger."

"You are so stupid, Oliver," Erica replied. "So, were you hallucinating or not?"

"No, but one time I was completely sober watching TV when it suddenly turned off, and then two hours later... it turned back on without me even touching the remote. Then, I ended up missing the ending to the second episode of "Back to the Future" before watching the third episode, and that was way more fucked up than smoking weed."

"Oh, my God," Erica replied. "I can't believe I'm in love with you. You are such a goober."

"That really happened," I said, looking at my fingers. "Now, how many is that?"

"I don't know," Erica answered. "I lost track."

"Well, it's a lot."

"Okay, give me one good reason... and I mean one really good reason why I should smoke weed... and maybe I will smoke some with you today."

"Because you would never know what it felt like if you never tried it!" I answered, not even thinking through this response. Nevertheless, it was both clever and convincing.

"That is a pretty good reason, actually," Erica said, after a suspenseful internal debate. "Okay, I will take just one hit." The first hit Erica took, she blew out quickly as if she only wanted to taste it rather than smoke it.

"No, that's not how you take a hit of weed," I said, grabbing the joint back. "Here, let me show you... take a big hit and hold it in." Erica then took a much bigger hit and tried her best to hold it in. At this point, I watched her face turn red as she began coughing so hard that she ran over to the side of the sunflower field and puked. I was laughing so hard at this point that I almost puked myself.

"How was it?" I asked, as I watched Erica wrinkle her face and grab her stomach.

"I hate you," Erica said. "Oh my God!"

"Why?" I asked, laughing my ass off. "You just said that you loved me."

"Oh my God."

"What, what do you feel?"

"Oh my God, Oliver... holy shit!"

"What?"

"I am so fucking stoned!"

Erica said these words like they fell from the fluffiest cloud in the sky and started doing jumping jacks. Immediately after they were spoken, she laughed uncontrollably for the next several minutes.

When Erica's belly roll laughter finally paused, I looked at her and said, "Now, look at the butterflies and tell me they don't look a hell of a lot more kick-ass!"

A few days before school started, I remember a particularly pleasant afternoon. Erica and I had come to our favorite spot in the country and were once again enjoying the shade from the barn, lying on our backs and looking up at the sky. The grass was so green and soft where we were lying. This may have been the only patch of grass like this around for miles because it hadn't rained for a few weeks, and it was hotter than hell outside that day.

Erica seemed to use warm weather as a good excuse for taking her top off. I thought it was so sexy to see Erica's titties so freely exposed in the middle of nowhere. I remember Erica picking a dandelion as we lay there. When she blew the pedals off, they circled in the air above us for a moment before being carried off by a slight summer breeze. This same little breeze must have caught her nipples just right because she said, "Whooo... that was a little nippily."

I think the reason Erica liked to take her top off mainly was because it was hot outside, and it just felt good, but there were definitely times her shirt came off specifically to turn me on. It was hard for me to know the difference, but seeing her naked tits jiggling around always turned me on, regardless of her intentions. Erica didn't necessarily need to have her top off to make me horny. I wanted to have sex with her pretty much every day of my life, but this was not my decision. It drove me up the wall that she planned to wait untill an unspecified time in the future to have sex.

Erica protected her virginity like a nun on Sunday, but she was not shy when it came to sexual favors. I remember spending hours lying on our backs in the shade, learning how to pleasure each other. I'm not sure if it was pure natural talent or if she was just a quick learner, but I didn't have to give Erica much instruction. Conversely, Erica needed to explain damn near everything to me, it seemed. In hindsight, I appreciate how candid she was about this. In any case, this was one of the days Erica spent lying on her back with a wet pussy and a meticulous list of instructions.

"Do you know where my clit is?" Erica asked.

"Of course I do. It's inside your pussy somewhere."

"You're not wrong about that, I guess," Erica replied. "Do you have any idea how many times you have made me orgasm?"

"Like how many times this week?" I asked as I started to count on my fingers how many times I perused this sexual endeavor.

"Let's start there."

"Well, there were three times in my bedroom and once in yours. This is the second time we came out here, so if you want another orgasm today, that will be six times."

"Guess again, Oliver."

"Umm... it's got to be at least four times."

"Keep guessing."

"Three?"

"Nope?"

"Two?"

"Uhaha," Erica said, shaking her head back and forth.

"I only made you orgasm once!" I yelled out with shocking surprise.

"Oliver, I hate to tell you this, but you have only made me cum once this entire summer."

"Oh my God, what's wrong with you?"

This was the beginning of a long journey that has never reached a final destination. I have spent my entire life trying to figure out how to make women happy, and I still get thrown curveballs almost daily. Fortunately, I figured out how to pleasure Erica, but understanding her emotional intelligence was far more challenging.

I thought that after Erica taught me how to make her orgasm, this was going to lead to sex, but I was wrong about this, too. Erica and I were both seventeen years old, and almost every kid in high school was having sex by this age. It didn't bother me that I wasn't having sex, but it was challenging at times to understand my boundaries.

"Your turn," Erica said, after four straight hours of instructional pussy licking.

"Are you ready to have sex now?" I asked.

"No, Oliver, I will let you know when I'm ready," Erica said. "You ask me this two or three times a month, and it's starting to get annoying."

"I'm sorry."

"Don't be sorry. Just be respectful," Erica replied. "Now, do you want a blow job or not? I have to be home for dinner by six o'clock. That means that we have to leave here in about five minutes.

"Of course I do, but since I can't ask if you want to have sex anymore, will you at least tell me why?"

"I think that I have told you this before, but the reason that I won't have sex with you is because I don't want to get pregnant.

I also want to be absolutely sure that you will support my pro-life decision if you do happen to get me pregnant."

"But there are condoms and a million other ways to prevent pregnancy," I replied.

"Getting pregnant is not the only reason I don't want to have sex with you, Oliver. It is just one of several," Erica explained. "I am also waiting for exactly the right time. I just think I will enjoy it more later in life. I just want to take things one step at a time."

"Do you think that you are going to wait till you get married to have sex?"

"I seriously doubt it, but who knows," Erica replied. "I guess you are just going to have to wait and see. It doesn't make any difference if I decide to have sex with you tomorrow, the next day, or on my wedding day... eventually, you're gonna get laid."

I looked at her with my eyes wide open after she said this because I thought it was incredibly cool to hear her say such a profound statement about our future with such certainty. I felt the same way about her, and she knew it. I was not confused about my love for Erica, and she was not confused about her love for me. However, plenty of other things in life kept us confused about love in general, and these things certainly were not going to be figured out that afternoon.

Chapter VI

ONCE I REACHED THE end of my high school senior year, it felt like nothing was left to think about. Inside my head, I wasn't just graduating from high school; I was graduating from thinking altogether. I wish I could have continued with this thoughtless strive for the rest of my life. I would wait for an eternity to expire to regain this feeling of clarity.

Our class really got into the school spirit just before we graduated, and we celebrated this by having keg parties every night of the week. These parties took place at all sorts of random places in and around Ogallala. Some parties took place at some kid's house or family farm whose parents went away for the weekend, and some took place in a random field or in a deserted barn in the country. Others would be out at Lake McConaughy or near the Platte River, but most of us didn't really care where the party was. It didn't matter if they popped off in the country or in town, as long as there was booze and no adults around, we came to party.

This carefree mindset and mechanical drunkenness continued right through the night before our high school graduation ceremony. While on the way to this party, Erica and I found ourselves driving down a wet, muddy road near the Platte River. I borrowed my father's pick-up truck because I was warned that a four-wheel drive was needed to reach the destination. This venue was probably selected because everybody knew there was only one four-wheel-drive police vehicle in the entire town of Ogallala, and one cop couldn't bust us all.

This was a well-thought-out plan, except that several vehicles ended up getting parked along the road where the ruts and mud got too deep. While on the way out to the party, Erica and I found a group of people standing around where all these vehicles were parked. Adam and Eric happened to be amongst this group of teenagers who didn't get the memo. They drove out together, thinking they would make it to the party in Eric's compact car.

When I pulled up in my dad's four-wheel-drive truck, they both hopped in the cab with Erica and I, while the other kids jumped in the back of the truck. Then, we all continued to the party down a road where rednecks traveled to attain a strange fix and test their most recent theory about mud. We drove around looking for the party bonfire on the bank of the Platte River for about thirty minutes. During this time, I listened to a new CD and rolled down the windows so everyone riding along could hear it. After listening to eight Hank Williams III songs about getting drunk when his dog ran away, when his mama died, and when his pa went to prison, I'm surprised we were able to celebrate anything... even the end of our senior year.

The party was in full swing when we finally found the bonfire and the drunk kids standing beside it. Country music was already being played by whoever had the loudest stereo in their truck, the hottest girls in class were already getting laid by the luckiest guys in school, and red cups were already getting filled with keg beer. Everyone in our senior class was really celebrating their asses off.

I remember seeing one kid that was already shitfaced, hammered drunk when we arrived. He was holding two red cups in his hands while I stood in line to get my first beer. This guy was undoubtedly the drunkest person at the party. He might have been the most drunken person in the world that night. At one point, this kid was running around naked, listening to Burning Ring of Fire by Johnny Cash. Apparently, he felt so inspired by this song that he actually tossed himself into the burning ring of fire. It may have been an ordinary bonfire to the rest of our class, but it was nothing short of a country music biblical revelation to him.

I couldn't help but wonder what was going through this guy's head when he did this. Perhaps he thought, "My entire life has been absolutely meaningless up until this point, and I really want my classmates to understand this." It's also possible that he was so drunk that he didn't know what the hell he was doing and thought nothing at all. The thing is... he would wake up the next morning after being blacked out drunk and have the most bitchin' hangover of his life thus far. He would have no idea how he got home, how his body got burned in so many places, or why he smelled like burnt hair and bonfire smoke. He would probably order himself a pizza and have absolutely no recollection of being a class clown jackass or the two-fisted red-cup guy. His embarrassment and integrity would just get sealed in a blackout vault until the next time there was a party with an opportunity to do something incredibly stupid. Whether he would get invited or not, it was guaranteed that he would be there fulfilling his civic duties as the two-fisted, red-cup drunk guy because that was just the kind of person he was.

As many problems as this guy would have in life, he certainly wasn't the only person at that party with problems. The fact is that every person who attended that party would eventually learn that nobody is perfect. It was all but guaranteed that each one of us would run around naked and toss ourselves into the bonfire of life someday. Hopes and dreams would come and go, but we'd all get burnt eventually. Fortunately, we didn't have to think about that as a teenager. As a matter of fact, we didn't have to think of anything at all. We were young, wild, and free to do whatever the hell we wanted.

Some of us would remain friends as the years passed, and some of our best friends in high school we would never see again after graduating. High school sweethearts would eventually get married, but not likely to each other. We all would one day learn that love is unpredictable and cannot be managed. It was inevitable that the greatest sadness in each of our lives would likely occur when a particular relationship struggles for the last time. Most of us would eventually realize that the loneliest feeling of desolation usually comes from painful sentiments of love, but we didn't know this yet.

At this point in our lives, none of us knew how hard life really was. Nobody was an alcoholic or a drug addict because we all were at the same party, drinking the same booze and passing around the same joints. None of us were married, so none of us could get a divorce. A lousy economy couldn't result in a layoff from a job we really liked or a foreclosure on a house we thought we'd live in forever. We didn't have jobs that mattered to us yet, nor did anyone own a home, but it was inevitable that each one of us would lose something that we thought would be around forever, but we didn't know this yet.

Most of our parents were still too young to die from an illness caused by old age, but they would eventually get cancer, suffer heart attacks, and their kidneys would fail. Some of them would survive these ailments, and some would die, but it was guaranteed that someday in the future, we would all know what it feels like to put flowers next to their tombstone, we just didn't know it yet.

Some of us would have a happy marriage with beautiful wives and handsome husbands. Others would never get married at all. Some of us would have children with two loving parents, and others would have children with someone they only met once. The rest of us would think about what it would be like to have children. There would be abortions, miscarriages, unplanned pregnancies, and still-born babies. Some of us would become a single mother, a single father, or even deadbeat parents. We all would toil with relationships and thoughts about children no matter what our future marital status would be, we just didn't know it yet.

Plenty of us planned to go to college, and some of us were simply happy to graduate high school. This was as far as any of us could see into our futures at this time in our lives. The world wasn't ready to cast shade onto our decisions, and there was no such thing as failure because the story of our lives was just beginning. This was the most incredible time in our entire life, but we didn't know this yet... we didn't know a goddamn thing. That was what made this time in our lives beautiful, and when we eventually realized this, we would know all too well.

Erica and I would graduate the following day. However, I didn't celebrate graduation like other kids in my class. It wasn't that I didn't appreciate finishing twelve years of education, I just didn't see the point in prolonging a celebration that had been going on since halfway through my senior year. I wasn't involved in high school sports, extracurricular activities, or anything found to be admirable by fellow alumni. As far as I was concerned, this seemed to render my graduation ceremony pointless. The bottom line is that I wasn't interested in standing on stage with my diploma alongside a bunch of people whom I absolutely hated.

Many of the kids in my class may have forgotten about the days when Erica and I would turn to each other in tears from constant torment by our peers. They constantly picked on us for smelling like cow shit and wearing dirty clothes from farm work that often began hours before the school bell rang. Almost every kid I graduated with punched me in the face at least once while growing up, and about half of them seemed to make this a habit through our first year in high school. Little did they know that I would eventually get even during our freshman year when I secretly hid under our homecoming float and set it on fire during the middle of the parade.

I felt this was enough for most of my class, but some kids deserved more than this collective act of revenge. For instance, our high school star quarterback stuck a firecracker up my ass and lit my hair on fire when I was twelve years old. Until we became sophomores, this jerk constantly picked on me and beat me up several times while I was growing up. I can't remember if I got up on the wrong side of the bed or if he spit on my lunch that day, but I finally decided that I wasn't going to take any more of his shit. All of my built-up rage after years of torment exploded in the high school locker room while he was getting ready for football practice. The entire football team watched as I beat the shit out of him with his own helmet. His teammates didn't know what to think of this and just stood around, picking their jaws up from the floor. After this experience, I was certain that hopeless fuck would never forget what he did to me or how he made me feel growing up. However, if he ever needed a reminder, I kept his helmet as a keepsake just in case I needed to beat the shit out of him with it again someday.

Another example was in the fourth grade when four kids took off Erica's clothes in the middle of winter on a subzero day. Then they threw her head face-first into a snowbank while we waited for her mom to bring us home from school. If it wasn't for my winter jacket, Erica could have frozen to death that day because her mother was dealing with a flat tire and was almost two hours late to pick us up. I reminded them of this one by one during the winter of my sophomore year by doing to them what they did to Erica. If it wasn't for my kind heart, these four hopeless, brainless pieces of shit would be dead right now rather than graduating high school with their lame-ass friends.

There was another time that I blew up a truck owned by the tallest kid in our school. It only took sixteen sticks of dynamite to make that bastard wish that he never made me eat dog shit in the third grade, hung me from the monkey bars by my underwear in the fifth grade, or tied my hands behind my back before pushing me over and pissing on my head in the sixth grade. After three years of watching that asshole drive around drunk, squealing his tires, and running over little kids' bikes for the fun of it, I enjoyed myself thoroughly when I lit a ten-foot fuse that resulted in an explosion so spectacular that a chunk of his motor came screaming through history class 101's window almost a block away. The blast shook the school so hard it caused a two-inch crack in one of the walls. Since school was let out early that day, I thought everyone in high school secretly owed me a favor, and I planned to cash in on each of these favors one by one.

While attending school for twelve long years, I acquired some unique enemies and a handful of incredible friendships. This balancing of friends and foes was interesting, to say the least. I hated hard and loved hard and had no idea how to gracefully express or balance these two crown chakra emotions while living in Ogallala. I was not meant for this place, so I had no interest in participating in my high school graduation ceremony.

I told my parents several times during my senior year that I had planned to do a lot of traveling after graduation. Knowing this, they gave me a suitcase and some money for my graduation present. This is when I got a hair up my ass and decided I was going to move to California. I started packing my suitcase to move a week later. Once my suitcase was filled with clothes, notebooks, trinkets, and pictures of Erica, I tossed it in my 1995 Honda Civic, along with some pillows and blankets.

Then, I started driving around town, saying goodbye to all my friends, which didn't take long because there were only four. When I was finished saying goodbye to everyone but Billy, I went to see several other kids I knew. These were people who were happy as hell to see me leaving because we absolutely hated each other. I just wanted to tell them that I hoped they failed in life, and I never planned to see them again. Finally, I went to see Billy. Our conversation was brief.

"Yo dude. What's up?".

"Nothing," Billy responded. "What's up with you?"

"I guess I'm moving ... so what do you plan to do when I leave?"

"I plan to smoke pot with your girlfriend," Billy answered.

"No, I mean really... what are your plans?"

"I don't know, man. I guess I'll just keep on being me. It will suck not having you around, but I will try to keep my head up," Billy said with a somber tone. "What are you planning to do in California?"

"Do shit, I guess." Suddenly, realizing that I didn't have any friends where I was going. "Dude, I'm going to miss you."

"No, you won't," Billy replied. "All that you are going to miss about Nebraska is Erica's sweet ass, and you know it."

"I will miss other things about Nebraska, too."

"Like what?" Billy asked.

"Like... fishing and hunting... and I'll miss my pals, especially you. You are right about the fact that I will miss Erica and her sweet ass, though."

"Speaking of Erica's sweet ass... is she available?"

"Fuck you, Billy."

"Hey, don't go away mad... just go away."

"I'm not mad," I said. "You're just a dick."

"Hey, you know I'm kidding," Billy said. "If anything, I make sure the usual crowd of fuckboys keep their distance."

"I appreciate that," I replied. "Maybe you can come visit."

"Hell yeah! I hear the chicks out in Cali are fine as hell. I could go for a bikini babe or two."

"That sounds about right," I replied. "Seriously, I'm going to miss you."

"I'll miss you too, Oliver."

"Well, see ya later, I guess."

"Stay gold, Ponyboy... stay gold."

Ponyboy,

I asked the nurse to give you this book so you could finish it. It's worth saving those little kids. Their lives are worth more than mine. Tell Dally I think it is worth it. I'm going to miss you guys. I have been thinking about it. In that poem... the guy that wrote it. He meant that you are gold when you are a kid. When you are a kid, everything is new. Like the way you dig sunsets, Pony... that's gold. Keep it that way. It's a good way to be. I want you to ask Dally to look at one. I don't think he has ever seen a sunset. There is still a lot of good in the world. Tell Dally that I don't think he knows.

Your buddy, Johnny

The Outsiders, SE Hinton 1967

I returned to my house around noon to eat lunch and say good-bye to my parents. The conversation between my parents and me was pretty brief as well. I told them my immediate plans and discussed what I hoped to accomplish by moving to the West Coast. In all actuality, I had no plans and wasn't expecting to accomplish much of anything. I didn't even have any real destination in mind yet.

"Are you actually leaving?" my dad asked.

"Yeah, I guess so. It is probably about time I figure out what I want to do with my life."

"When are you planning to leave, Oliver?" my mom asked.

"Shortly."

"Are you planning to leave today?"

"Yeah," I answered. "I really want to get going."

"Why don't you leave tomorrow?" my mom asked with a look of concern.

"I just want to get on the road."

"Where are you going to sleep tonight?"

"I have packed my car just right to put the back seats down. Between the back seat and the trunk, I will have plenty of room to stretch out and rest comfortably."

"I don't know about that... it sounds pretty dangerous to me," my mother said.

"No, Mom, it's not going to be dangerous," I replied. "You just think it will be dangerous because you have never been anywhere but Ogallala."

"You better talk to your father about this."

"Just let him go, for crying out loud. He is eighteen and can do what he wants to," my father said, not even looking away from the TV.

While I was walking out the door, my mother stopped me to hug me with tears in her eyes. This was followed by a handshake from my father, who stood beside the door.

"Congratulations, son, you are moving away just like you planned last week. Try not to make an ass out of yourself out there in Yuppyville, California."

"I'll try my best."

"I'm sure you will, son, and even if you do make an ass out of yourself, it won't matter because California is full of communist bastards... except for Arnold Schwarzenegger... I love that guy. If you happen to see him while you are out there, make sure to tell him that your dad said hi. "I'll be back," my dad said, giving his best impression of his favorite actor.

"Okay, Dad, I will."

"Be careful, Oliver," my mom said, as I started to walk out the front door.

"I will, Mom... don't worry."

"Wear your seat belt, and make sure to call us."

"Okay, Mom, I'll call you when I get to wherever I'm going."

"I love you."

"I love you, too."

I acknowledged that leaving Erica was the one thing about my departure that made no sense. I spent the next few hours begging her to come with me, but I knew that I was beating a dead horse to death.

I told her that I was moving to California only a week earlier, acting on an immature whim, not really thinking how it would affect our relationship. The irony was that I planned to spend the rest of my life with Erica.

"Oliver, before you go, I want to tell you something," Erica said.

"What's that?"

"I know that you are a virgin."

"How did you know that?"

"I didn't," Erica explained, "but I do now."

"Oh my God, really?"

"Yes, really, but today is your lucky day. I may not be able to change your plans to move to the West Coast, but I can make you move back home in a quick hurry."

"How do you plan to do that?"

"Stand here for a minute. I'll be right back." I did what I was told and spent the next minute or so looking around Erica's room without a clue. When she returned to her room, she was wearing a black lace Victoria's Secret corset, fishnet stockings, and a mesh garter belt over the smallest pair of G-string panties I had ever seen.

"Do you like what you see, Oliver?" Erica asked, as she did a little twirl.

"Wow, you look incredible."

"What do you think about these panties?"

"You're wearing panties?"

"I sure am," Erica said, with a seductive smile, "and it sounds like I am getting my money's worth."

For the next several minutes, I watched Erica dance around me, trying her very hardest to look as sexy as possible. Erica could have been wearing a winter coat, and she would have still given me an erection. I had never seen Erica wear lingerie before. As a matter of fact, I had never seen her wear anything but blue light special bras and panties.

After she finished her little dance, she dropped down to her knees and teased me with a series of several two-second blowjobs. She eventually laid down on the bed and pulled her tiny little panties over to her inner thigh. Then, she used her pointer finger, gesturing me to come closer to a well-thought-out sexual fantasy.

"Do you think it's going to feel good?" Erica said seductively. At this point, I still didn't understand that she was planning to have sex with me.

"Do I think what will feel good?" I asked like an idiot.

Erica spent the next hour ensuring I knew exactly what she was talking about. By the time she was done with me, her goal was accomplished. I didn't know it yet, but I didn't stand a chance of becoming a resident of California. I was thinking of becoming a permanent resident of her bedroom and likely would have never even left Ogallala if Erica hadn't encouraged me to leave. I lost my virginity the same as she did that day, but for Erica, this wasn't all for pleasure.

I probably thought about having sex with Erica every day of my life for at least a decade after this experience. I didn't understand what just happened. I thought that Erica just wanted to have sex with me before I left for California. Erica knew that we were not going to have sex. She planned to make love, and that changed everything.

Chapter VII

A COUPLE OF HOURS after losing my virginity, I found myself driving down the road with music blaring into my ears, out my windows, and onto the flat land of western Nebraska. I had everything going for me at this moment in time. The world was my oyster... as they say. I was driving west with no idea where my future was headed. The only thing I was sure of was that I was traveling in the direction of a brilliant sunset, and that was all that mattered to me.

I was eighteen years old and wasn't scared of anything yet. There wasn't a single pain in my body, my heart was full of love, and my mind was high on marijuana. I had just started on this journey through life, and I was excited as hell about it. I felt so enthusiastic about life that I needed little rest during this trip to the West Coast.

The city lights of Denver and Las Vegas interrupted the darkness of night, while the light of day wasn't interrupted by anything but my sunglasses. My car sputtered over the Rocky Mountains of Colorado and through the desert of southern Nevada. I crossed through Death Valley so incredibly alive that my broken air conditioner didn't even seem broken. The intense heat just reminded me why I needed to get it fixed, is all.

I traveled down the busy Interstate 10 expressway outside Los Angeles until I hit a gridlock traffic jam. This didn't bother me at all. I just rolled down my windows and turned up the volume on my stereo. I remember listening to the song Black by Pearl Jam and pretending it was possible to understand Eddie Vedder's lyrics.

I was in the city of Angels for a few short hours before passing by a sign that caught my attention. Venice Beach was only five miles away. The sign said that this city had a population of 37,000 people. I was sure that these would be my kind of people... the freaks... the weirdos... the confidently misinformed, and now me. I drove into this city with a purpose and plan to fulfill my hopes and dreams. I was here to start a new life, hoping to discover an identity beyond the boundaries of rural living and parental guidance.

I was convinced that everything in life would be perfect living here. My opinion of this place was that it was exotic and fun. I had little or no reservations about living in SoCal and didn't think it would be possible for my opinion to change. I rented a surfboard to experience the waves in the Pacific Ocean and bought a skateboard to roll down the sidewalk between the beach and the city. I walked up and down and around Venice Beach streets, looking for new friends and new experiences. My mind was young, and my thoughts were innocent. It felt like I had a plan for everything, and my current goal in life was to experience something psychedelic and meaningful ... all I needed to do now was find some LSD.

I met Fredrick four days after arriving in Venice Beach. He was walking barefoot down the sidewalk adjacent to the beach. He had dreadlocks in his hair and hippy on his clothes, so I figured this man had plenty of hallucinogenic drugs to share with me. I would one day learn not to judge people by their appearance. This particular person didn't teach me this lesson because Fredrick happened to have an awful lot of LSD in his pocket that day. More importantly, he wasn't just willing to sell me a hit or two. He was excited to share whatever it took to hang out and experience a good acid trip.

"Hey man, you wouldn't happen to have some acid, would you?" I asked, enthusiastic and hopeful.

"Sure do!" Fredrick responded as he reached into his pocket and pulled out a sheet of high-quality LSD. "How many hits do you want?"

"How much does it cost?" I asked.

"Depends on how much you want."

"Two or three, I guess."

"Two or three sheets, or two or three hits?" he asked.

"I just want to trip, is all."

"Well, do you take a hit when you trip, or do you take a sheet when you trip?"

"I have never eaten acid before," I confessed. "What do you recommend?"

"If it's your first time, I'd recommend a ten strip, I suppose," Fredrick said, completely out of touch with the reality and temperament of your average drug user. "I tell you what, I'm just going to rip a corner off of this sheet and give it to you in celebration of your first acid trip," Fredrick said.

"Really?" I asked, feeling super excited.

"Sure, buddy," he responded with a funny-looking grin. "I'll even trip out with you... it will be fun!"

"That sounds awesome! My name is Oliver."

"I'm Fredrick, nice to meet you."

This is how I met my first friend in Venice Beach. I asked to buy a recommended dose of LSD for a first-time user, and I was handed a ten-strip for free. I would learn a lot during the next twenty-four hours. One thing I would learn in particular is that a ten strip of acid is a massive dose for first-time users and, generally speaking, for anyone seeking a standard hallucinogenic drug experience. This was particularly true with any LSD Fredrick had. What he gave me that day was authentic reissued triple-dipped Timothy Leary blotter acid. A single hit of this acid would send your average person to the moon.

Ten hits would create the possibility of visiting another galaxy or contacting some dead relatives. When you were finished with this psychedelic experience, you'd likely think the conversation you had with your dead relatives was entirely hallucinogenic. There would also be a solid chance you just had an insightful conversation with your grandma. This is how good this LSD was. There was no telling where it was going to take you.

I have only tripped on acid a few dozen times, but this was enough to learn that what you see in front of you right now is what tangible reality and your current headspace are allowing you to see. However, what is actually in front of you is infinitely more complicated to explain. The wonders of the universe are not limited to three dimensions, and your brain is not limited to standard thoughts. I am convinced that infinite possibilities exist within this equation. If you have never eaten acid in your life for whatever reason you may have, I would highly recommend that you go looking for your own Fredrick to trip balls with at least once in your life.

My acid trip was everything I thought it would be and more. I hallucinated and laughed so hard that I nearly puked. Fredrick and I shared belly-roll laughter repeatedly while the sun set over the Pacific Ocean. I laughed at many random things because the acid made everything funny, and Fredrick mostly just laughed at me. I saw shapes and colors I had never seen before. It was a fantastic experience! We walked around all night, looking into space and feeling the stars.

Fredrick lived only two blocks from the main road parallel to the ocean. He lived alone with his dog in a big four-bedroom apartment and invited me over as we began to come down from our trip. At one point, I asked Fredrick what he did for a living. He responded with laughter and a goofy hippy smile. I figured out pretty quickly that he sold drugs for a living. He also told me about his lucrative hobby. He had a kiln set up in one of his bedrooms, which was used to harden the glass pipes he blew. We got along really well for some reason. I liked Fredrick, and he liked me.

I ended up crashing on Fredrick's couch in an extra bedroom for a week as he talked about leaving for Washington to go to a Phish concert. I had never even heard of this band before and wasn't familiar with any hippy band or the culture that came with it. Fredrick found all this intriguing and made me listen to a lot of Phish and the Grateful Dead during that week. I was having so much fun drinking beers and smoking bowls without a care in the world that I didn't even know that I was being groomed into the life of a hippy.

Fredrick asked if I wanted to join him as he traveled to Washington to attend this concert. I thought long and hard about it before agreeing to go with him. One week to the day after arriving on the West Coast, I climbed into Fredrick's red hippy van along with his big, friendly dog and left southern California. Our destination would be new and exciting regardless of where this place was on the map. We took Highway 101 up the coast until we hit Monterrey Bay. At this point, I thought Fredrick was doing me a favor by including San Francisco in our journey.

I was about sixty miles in the wrong direction, but it was worth the trip, at least. Fredrick paid for a hotel. Then we ate dinner and breakfast at the Fisherman Wharf. I fell in love with San Fransisco Bay the moment I arrived there. After seeing so many pictures growing up, I realized that the Golden Gate Bridge was fantastic to see in person.

From there, we drove through Portland and had lunch before continuing to Seattle. This was another place that we didn't need to travel to as it was not directly on the way to the Gorge Amphitheatre. We ate at Pikes Market and stayed the night a few blocks away.

We finally arrived at our destination on the third day of travel, and it felt like we were in the middle of nowhere because you could not see the actual venue until you got into the parking lot. This process took all afternoon, but we eventually found a spot to park the van and set up a large tent. There were thousands of hippies camping out near the amphitheater. It truly was a sight to see.

There were no restaurants or bars in this temporary village, but there was every type of food, drink, and chemical known to man in this place if you just looked around. Fredrick set up a table for all his glass pipes, along with a sign that said LSD for sale. I knew he had brought acid with us to sell, but it wasn't till he offered me a few sheets to sell that I realized just how much acid he had brought.

Fredrick had three or four hundred sheets of gel tabs in assorted colors. That is forty-thousand hits of acid for those who know nothing about this drug. There are some interesting things about this statistic beyond the sheer volume of acid Fredrick was bringing to this concert. Roughly twenty thousand people would attend this concert, so that means that Fredrick alone could supply enough acid for everyone at that concert to trip, assuming they all had first-time user tolerance levels. With this said, the tolerance level of the average fan-goer at a Phish concert was considerably higher than this, mainly because there were likely a handful of people like Fredrick who could eat an entire sheet of acid over a couple of days.

The other interesting thing about this statistic was that at least a couple dozen more fan-goers brought this much acid to the concert. In addition, there were likely a couple hundred people who also brought at least a sheet with them and hundreds who brought a personal supply. If you were to add this up, you'd find that there would be roughly one million hits of acid at this concert.

This wasn't just some run-of-the-mill acid either. This concert took place during an era of about three years when the quality of LSD was exceptionally high. I'm pretty sure these gel tabs were close to the best hits of acid ever known to man. There were also hits called microdots and genuine reissue Timothy Leary blotter acid that was also around at the time. A couple of years after this concert took place, this era of time would be over, and it would be unusual to find anything but blotter paper and liquid LSD.

Fredrick ended up selling me three of the sheets of acid that he had for a few hundred dollars, and I was about to sell two of these sheets in smaller quantities for about 750 dollars while I was attending this three-day festival. This left me with a personal supply of one hundred hits and padded the amount of money that I currently was living on.

One of the most intriguing things I saw at the festival was this 1980 orange Pinto, which was completely full of hallucinogenic mushrooms. There were several trash bags sitting around this car with signs sticking out of them that said "1/8th for $10." That blew my mind! I mean, nobody gave a rat's ass about anything in this place. There were zero laws and little logic to follow when seeking answers to this gigantic three-day hippy festival.

During the days, I helped Fredrick sell glass and acid. Then, we would go to the concerts at night. I ate mushrooms one night and ate acid another. On the last day, I got piss drunk and danced around with some cute hippy chicks at the concert. That was my favorite night. I wasn't really into the music all that much. It was good, but I wouldn't buy an album or anything.

Just before we started our journey back to Venice Beach, Fredrick continued to surprise me by purchasing the remaining two giant trash bags full of mushrooms that the Pinto car had left. I thought this was an awful lot to travel with back to southern California, but he didn't seem to think so. He just loaded these trash bags full of mushrooms into his van along with his glass pipes and his big, friendly dog like it was not a big deal at all.

After we were all ready and packed to leave, getting out of this venue was quite the spectacle, just as it was to get in. It's a wonder that we even made it out the gate that day because there were twenty thousand hippies stoned out of their minds while coming down from a three-day psychedelic drug experience. It took so long for us to get out of the amphitheater that we only made it to Olympia before stopping to find a hotel.

We continued south the following day until we arrived in Humboldt County, where my mind was about to get blown once again. Fredrick wouldn't warn or prepare me before going on these random little adventures, and this particular one was absolutely bonkers. It was almost as mind-blowing as the entire three-day Phish extravaganza.

We drove over some hills and down gravel roads until we arrived at a massive grow operation. Now, when I say massive, I literally looked out onto fields and rolling hills of marijuana that went on for miles. It was just like driving across the farmland of eastern Nebraska and looking out onto miles of sunflowers, wheat, or corn.

This was only half of what blew my mind. At least fifty, if not more than a hundred, people were working at this farm. I saw piles of weed as big as a small house. I swear to you, this place existed. Anyway, we spent a night here drinking and smoking with a bunch of hippies before leaving the following day with eight trash bags of weed in addition to the two trash bags of hallucinogenic mush-rooms.

At this point, the dog and I barely fit in the van. I won't lie, I was a little freaked out about this. I mean, I saw Billy with a shit ton of weed at times, but never this much. Also, this van was not exactly a stealth vehicle. I mean, it actually looked like a hippy van full of drugs. It was a very well-maintained vehicle that resembled the Volkswagen van you'd see in pictures of from the Woodstock era.

It was bright red with tie-dye curtains in the windows and Grateful Dead bear stickers on the bumper.

When we'd leave a convenience store or hotel, I'd immediately smell all this weed the moment I walked out the door, regardless of how far away the van was parked. It's not like you can hang an air freshener in the window to eliminate the smell of eight trash bags of kind bud. There was one instance when we walked out the wrong door of a large Holiday Inn and realized that Fredrick parked the van clear on the other side of the hotel. Even this distance of three hundred yards or more wasn't enough to clear the air.

It felt like Fredrick and his van were basically an illegal dumpster fire traveling down Highway 101 with a heightened risk appetite that would rival Hunter S. Thomson leaving Las Vegas with his attorney. There was something about the absolute zero fucks that Fredrick seemed to give that led me to think that he was wearing a hippy shield of some kind to keep the highway patrol off our tail. I didn't say anything about my general feeling of paranoia while we traveled, but I wanted to ask how the holy hell he felt so relaxed about this bizarre journey. It appeared that this gigantic elephant in the room was never a thought that crossed Fredrick's mind. He drove back to southern California, playing hippy music and chewing on sheets of acid while caring less than any man should about the fact his van was filled top to bottom with drugs.

When we finally arrived in Venice Beach after three full days of travel, I helped Fredrick bring these trash bags of drugs into his home. Then we drank a few beers and ordered a pizza while watching some reruns of Cheers like this was an everyday occurrence. I couldn't believe what I just experienced over the past couple of weeks. My thoughts about this crazy hippy adventure were both fantastic and frightening, which left me exhausted in a way that had nothing to do with sleep. Nevertheless, this experience finally ended with sweet dreams and a full night's rest.

I decided to leave the following day and exchanged a heartfelt goodbye with the enigma of Fredrick. Before I left that morning, I realized that this man was the most interesting person I had ever met. After all my crazy adventures with him, I considered him a dear friend and truly hoped this somber departure would not be the last time we would see each other. I finally parted ways, not knowing what day it was or where I was going. I just cleared off all the parking tickets left on my car and started to drive into the great unknown.

This departure initially felt meaningful, as if I was embarking on a journey to discover more adventures. I felt sad, happy, and puzzled as I began driving north on Highway 101 without any destination in mind. However, I only made it about ten miles before a deep feeling of loneliness began to bother me, like I was in a room full of misguided people who were all lost, abandoned, and paranoid. I had never felt anything like this in my life, and it caused an unfamiliar pain in my chest that hurt so bad that I couldn't drive anymore.

I remember getting out of my car and walking to the ocean while bawling my eyes out. There weren't any complete thoughts that were initially connected to this pain, but this lonely feeling eventually caused me to miss my family and friends in the weirdest way imaginable. This was more than just an unpleasant emotion. It was a wicked sensation so profoundly awkward that it felt like I had somehow deviated from my greater purpose in life.

After spending several minutes with my head in my hands and tears in my eyes, I suddenly began to understand this melancholy experience. This is when I realized that my purpose in life was to love Erica, and I couldn't do that if I were fifteen hundred miles away from her. Within minutes of this realization, I stopped crying and abruptly abandoned my West Coast adventure. This was when I looked out at the ocean one last time to say farewell. Then, I walked back to my car and drove for the next eighteen hours, feeling absolutely certain that the most beautiful place in the world was wherever Erica stood.

Chapter VIII

As I crossed the border into Nebraska, I began searching for a way to explain why I returned home so quickly. I wanted to provide a valid excuse to tell everyone so my conviction to move to the West Coast didn't look like a failure. Except for one conversation with Erica before I left to go to the Phish Concert, I had not talked to anyone from my hometown, so nobody knew about my West Coast experience or that I was coming back home.

For the past eighteen hours, I had been thinking about the erotic goodbye that Erica and I exchanged before I left for the West Coast. These thoughts seemed to elevate a feeling of failure I didn't want to own or admit to anyone, especially Erica. A fundamental conflict is embedded into every romance, making it nearly impossible to explain how the mystery of love has changed one's mind. This is a secret of passion that no one can explain, and all lovers sometimes fall victim to this enigma.

I didn't want to tell Erica that she was the reason I decided to come home, but I also didn't want to lie to her. As I drove past the city limit sign of Ogallala, I had every intention of telling Erica the truth. To everyone else, I could lie, but I felt Erica needed to know why I was about to knock on her door. Aside from my empty bag of excuses and this moral dilemma, what I thought about the most on this drive back home was our erotic goodbye. I showed up on Erica's doorstep with the fantasy that no words would be exchanged and that we would instantly pursue passionate lovemaking the moment we saw each other. My heart raced as I rang her doorbell.

"Oliver... oh my god! What are you doing here?" Erica asked, as she threw her arms around me.

"I came to see you!" I welcomed this hug and appreciated it more than anyone could imagine.

"Are you just visiting, or are you moving back?" Erica asked, all excited.

"I don't know just yet," I responded. This was a ridiculous statement to make from where I stood. Looking into Erica's eyes, I had no intention of ever leaving her again. It felt like when Erica and I made out with each other for the first time up at the starry place when I told her that I had sex before. I didn't know what I was saying, and I didn't understand why I was saying it.

"Did things work out for you?"

"Kind of," I replied.

"Why are you back?" Erica asked, with a curious look on her face. "Are you planning to stay with me in Ogallala?"

Once again, I found myself at a loss for words. I really wanted to say that I missed her so much that I almost went insane. I probably should have said that I couldn't stand being away from her for another day, but what I ended up saying was, "I'm here to see you for now... I guess."

"Oh," Erica replied, rolling her eyes and looking down at her feet. The expression on her face was worth a million words. To put it briefly, she wanted me to tell her that I had come home forever. It was as if Michelangelo began to paint the walls of Erica's house with irony because this was exactly what I wanted to tell her. Unfortunately, it seemed as if my mouth suddenly disconnected from the part of my brain that made sense when I talked.

I felt my body, heart, and mind all walking in different directions as I said, "Yeah, I don't know what is going on right now, but for now, I am so glad to see you." After saying this total bullshit, I held out my arms, wanting desperately to embrace the love of my life, but I couldn't form the words Erica needed to hear. I couldn't give her the satisfaction. I was being an asshole and didn't understand why.

Erica didn't even want to hug me. There was no doubt that she was being overemotional, but I was the problem. Maybe she just needed to vent for a moment, but whatever it was, she was suddenly very upset with me. So, I asked her, "Erica, why don't you just come back with me to the West Coast?"

"I told you, Oliver. I need to stay here."

"Why?"

"Why... you know why! My dad is dying, we barely have any money in the bank, and my dad's pension isn't covering all these medical expenses. The money I make at the supermarket needs to go a long way right now."

"Where is your dad?" I asked. "Is he really doing that bad?"

"He is in the hospital," Erica replied, with an upset look on her face. "He just had another minor procedure done yesterday."

"What is wrong with him?"

"He needs a heart transplant."

"Wow! Now I understand. I am so sorry, Erica. I can't imagine what you are going through," I said empathically.

"Thanks," Erica replied. "It's been an emotional couple of months."

"Not to be disrespectful, but where do you find a heart?" I asked.

"It's nearly impossible," Erica explained. "You need to find someone who donates their organs when they die."

"But people die all the time, so there should be hearts lying around everywhere," I replied without sarcasm. This is just what came out of my mouth, so I guess I could put this statement in the pile of bullshit things I said that day as well.

"That is not even funny, Oliver. He is on a waiting list that is over a year long. If he even lives for that long, a heart transplant is well over a million-dollar surgery. Our family's insurance doesn't even come close to covering this type of expense. I don't know what to do. I took a picture of my dad and put it on a coffee can with a little sign explaining my dad's heart condition and set it next to the till at the supermarket. I thought I could raise money that way, but at best, I only see a couple of dollars in there when I come to work in the morning," Erica said, with a lot of sadness in her voice.

"Wow, that is pretty heavy to hear. I'm really sorry," I replied with sincere sadness. I imagined Erica looking in this can and only seeing a couple of dollars, and it nearly made me start crying. I had such a big, dumb, philosophical heart when it came to things like this. Regardless of whether Erica and I were getting along from this day forward, I made it a point to stop by the supermarket as often as possible when she wasn't working to put as much as I feasibly could afford in this can.

"You won't believe this, but I have been doing searches for hearts on illegal search engines," Erica explained with peculiar hesitation.

"Like the black market?" I asked, not knowing what the black market even was.

"Exactly like the black market," Erica responded.

"I never expected you'd ever do something like this. You won't even carry a joint in your pocket," I mentioned. "How illegal is this?"

"It depends on what you get caught doing, but I'm sure illegal heart transplants don't result in probation. Even if you somehow manage not to get caught, just about a million other things can go wrong. You not only need to find a place to find a heart, but you also need to find a heart surgeon to perform the transplant."

"Where do illegal hearts come from?" I asked.

"I have found them in the Far East, Mexico, and South America."

"I meant to ask, who do they come from?"

"Don't ask that question!" Erica shouted. "Don't ever ask that horrible question again!"

"I'm sorry. I'm just curious," I responded, thinking Erica had gotten legitimately upset with me. Then she continued to answer my question, so you can chalk this up to another thing I didn't understand about our conversation that day.

"They come from living fucking people, Oliver! Use your goddamned brain for once!" Erica said, as she began to bawl her eyes out.

I leaned over and held her in my arms, intending to embrace and mollify her sadness. However, Erica continued to reject my honest empathy and continued to cry. With tears rolling down her face, she explained the entire process to me.

"The cheapest heart I can find is $750,000, and it's in fucking V-la-di-vos-tok," Erica said, sounding out the word.

"Wow!" I replied, "Where in the hell is that... and how do you plan to come up with that much money?"

"Yeah, fucking wow! It's a giant city somewhere in eastern Russia, and our house is only worth $200,000, so I don't know how! But let's just say, by some fucking miracle, it suddenly began to rain money... I would need to figure out how to get this money into the hands of some of the world's most dangerous criminals. I would also have to map out how to get myself and my dad, who is currently bedridden, all the way around the whole fucking world! I've never even been on a plane before! I don't have much confidence that I'd even find my way through the Goddamned airport, let alone navigate my way through the city streets of V-la-di-vos-tok.... whatever the hell it's called. If I don't even know how to say the name of this city, how am I supposed to find my way to this stupid place? And, let's just say for shits and giggles that we don't get killed while on this super scary scavenger hunt, then the hoping and the praying starts. Not only would this be one of the world's most illegal operating tables, but a heart transplant is the most dangerous surgical procedure that anyone can have. They would need to cut open someone's chest and pull out their goddamn heart. Assuming this random person lived a healthy lifestyle and didn't suffer a heart attack themselves once they figured out that they were headed to the black market as an organ donor, this person's heart still needs to be inserted in my father's chest!"

"Holy shit!" I responded. "I had no idea that something like this would be so dangerous!"

"Oh, I am not even close to being done here, Oliver! It doesn't stop here, oh fucking no... people don't just jump right out of bed after a heart transplant. Assuming the surgery went well, we would still need to find a legitimate recovery hospital in Russia. If I actually were to secure a recovery bed somewhere, at that point, I would need to transport my unconscious father back through the city streets of V-la-di-vos-tok and then over to the hospital. I'm going to take a wild guess and say calling a cab isn't going to work in this situation. Oh my God, Oliver, think how shitty this would be!"

At that point, I just stood there shaking my head, looking at the love of my life bawl her eyes out. I was about to say something, but Erica continued...

"I'd spend a month in East Russia, hoping my dad lived and I didn't get robbed, raped, or killed in the meantime. Finally, we would begin our journey back home following the same shitty flight path around the whole fucking world again. We would board a flight in V-la-di-vos-tok and fly to Bangkok International, then fly to Hong Kong or Tokyo, then stateside to San Fransico or LA, then to Denver, and finally, we'd have to drive home to good old Ogallala, Nebraska."

"Jeeeeezzzz," I replied with legitimate terror in my expression. "You have put a lot of thought into this. It sounds horrible!"

I have spent the last three months planning for this, knowing inside my own heart that there is not a snowball's chance in hell that my dad will actually get a transplant. Unless the black market suddenly has a 50% off sale on human hearts, my dad is going die!"

"I am so sorry," I replied, not knowing what else to say. I knew Erica was really emotional about all this because this was the most I had ever heard her swear. She had a sailor mouth anyway, but this was abnormal even for her.

"There is more, Oliver."

"More... how much more can there be?" I asked.

"A lot more."

"Like what?"

"I don't think I am ready to tell you this right now."

"Why not?" I asked, wondering what else she could possibly tell me.

"You might get mad at me."

"I'd never get mad at you. What is it? Is it more stuff about your dad's heart?"

"Kind of," she answered.

"Just tell me. I promise not to get mad," I told her, now very curious about what she had to say.

"For me to get this information about the heart transplant and stuff, I needed to pay for it."

"How much money is it for information on heart transplants performed thousands of miles away?" I asked, expecting her to say it was fifty dollars.

"Oliver, these websites are super illegal, and the guy that gets me this information doesn't take cash," she responded, and then she began to start crying hard... really hard.

"What is wrong?" I asked. "Are you writing him bad checks or something?"

"Oliver, I'm trading him pictures of me."

"Pictures?" I replied. "That isn't so bad."

"They are if I am naked in those pictures," she said, crying her eyes out. "That isn't all of it either..."

"What the fuck, there is more?" I asked, not believing what I was hearing,

"Kind of a lot more," she said, while looking like she wanted to die.

"What else could there possibly be?" I asked, perplexed and angry.

"See this thing attached to my computer. It is a web camera," she explained, barely able to look at me or speak clearly. "He watches me put things inside me, and he keeps getting nastier and nastier each time... and I keep doing what he says... I keep doing what he says because he says I'm not worth anything once I turn eighteen... so I need to trade him a whole bunch of videos now because there is only one thing he is interested in after I turn eighteen, and I don't want to have to do it... I can't do it... I don't even know if it's possible to fit the things he is talking about in my asshole, and my birthday is in two weeks... and I don't want to get blacklisted from ever getting my dad a heart!"

After she said this, I could barely breathe. I experienced a void in my chest that didn't allow me to inhale. I sat there speechless for a minute or two before I completely lost my fucking mind. I started screaming at Erica about how fucked up I thought all this was and that I couldn't believe what she was doing!

"I thought you said you weren't going to get mad," Erica said. "I'm the one who should be mad! You tell me a week before you leave that you are moving to California, and then you come back, and now you don't know how long you'll be here. I'm the one who should be mad, not you!"

"I'm not the one that's putting things up my ass for a fucking stranger!" I yelled.

"I'm not going to do it!" she replied, while yelling and crying uncontrollably.

"Fuck almighty, Erica. What the holy hell were you thinking?"

"Stop yelling at me!" she demanded as if this were an option. "What do you expect me to do? My dad is fucking dying! Do you have any idea what I am going through right now? I don't have a family like everyone else. I don't have a brother or a sister here. My brother is stationed in the Middle East, and who knows when or if he is coming home…, and my mom died of brain cancer when I was thirteen. You don't know what I'm going through. My dad is the only family I have right now. What do you expect me to do?"

I didn't understand this question. My mind drifted into a type of rage that no longer allowed me to think… I was just raging. The only thing my mouth let me do at this point was yell, "FUCK!" at the top of my lungs.

"Do you want to break up with me?" she asked, completely misreading why I was angry. "Is that what you want?"

"No, I don't want to fucking break up with you!" I answered, screaming at the top of my lungs. My anger was not at her. It only appeared so because I didn't know how to keep my rage inside of me. I was angry at the world for putting her in this situation, but she didn't understand this, and I couldn't calm down enough to explain it. She was right. I didn't know what she was going through. There was no way to comprehend the pain she was feeling or the level of fear that led her to do this to herself. My heart was breaking into a million pieces because I loved her more than anything in the world. I wasn't just sad and angry about this… I was destroyed.

"Stop yelling!" she responded every time I opened my mouth. "What do you expect me to do?"

"I want to fucking kill that guy, and I want you to stop acting like a slut! That is whaaaaaaaa..." As this word came out of my mouth... time paused. I mean, the whole world just stopped fucking working for a few painful moments. I watched her face express a level of pain and embarrassment no words could describe. I didn't just call her a slut. I would never think that way about her, so I wouldn't ever call her that... but that was what had come out of my mouth. No matter how much my words were taken out of context and misunderstood, Erica was not going to solve the riddle of this extraordinary irony anytime soon.

Nearly a minute of horrifying silence followed this word. The room was so quiet that I could hear the tears falling from Erica's eyes. "I'm sorry," I said, breaking the eerie silence. "I didn't mean that."

"What did you mean to say?" Erica asked. I could tell by her voice how upset this had made her feel.

"I don't know what I meant," I replied. I felt horrible, and I was just scratching the surface of the mistake I had made. This wasn't just a poor choice of words. This was a life-changing narrative that could have potentially ended the most important relationship in my life.

"You think I'm a slut," she replied, as the sadness in her tears began to turn to anger.

"Don't say that!"

"Don't say what?" she asked, getting angrier by the second. "That I'm a slut... Is that it?"

"No, don't say anything," I answered, about to start crying myself.

"Listen closely, Oliver, because this will be the last thing you hear me say. Our relationship is officially fucking over!"

"Please, don't say that!"

"Leave," she said, as she walked over to the door and opened it. I stood in the doorway, trying to find a way to fix this.

"I'm really sorry," I replied, giving my best attempt at another apology.

Then she walked up to me and looked me straight in the eyes, "GET THE FUCK OUT OF MY HOUSE!"

I knew that if this horrifying wrinkle in time unraveled itself for long enough, I might never be forgiven. I walked back into Erica's room after she yelled at me, tore her computer off her desk, and walked out her front door with it. Erica didn't say or do anything to stop me either.

I had no clue what to do at this point. I didn't want to stay and make her angrier than she already was, yet I didn't want to leave her thinking I thought that she was slut either. I needed to find a way to rephrase and retract what had been said, but there needed to be so much more than an apology to reconcile our differences. A year and a half passed without us having any actual argument, but that all suddenly came to an end on this dreadful day. We just experienced our first fight, and an epic fight it was... holy shit! After Erica's front door had been shut, I stood on her doorstep, holding her computer and crying.

My entire world changed direction that day. I had no goals in life and no real direction besides my commitment to Erica up until then, but two goals in my life suddenly became clear. I was going to fix what had just happened. The bond Erica and I shared was so strong, and our love for each other was so deep that I didn't need to set any new relationship goals to make her happy. I needed to avenge her sadness. So, the first goal I ever made in my life was to figure out a way to pay for her father's heart transplant, and my second goal was to find the person who exploited Erica and seek revenge.

I went home from Erica's house, completely dumbfounded about what just happened. I had no idea how to handle this situation. I was crushed and ended up just staying in my room for the next several days. During this time, I wrote a poem and drew a picture, attempting to vent my melancholy. These activities helped but fell well short of being a cure. In fact, they may not have helped at all and could have brought this epic sadness more into focus. Regardless of how I was affected by this, my anxiety was at an all-time high. The feeling in my chest was painful, and not just metaphorically speaking. It was literally painful and a force to be reckoned with all day long.

Although the feeling of regret was driving me mad, some of my thoughts were even worse. What Erica had described to me was terrifying from any perspective, and I assumed the level of terror I experienced to be minor in comparison to hers. These thoughts transcended well beyond relationship trouble because they were more sinister and complex to process.

I walked off Erica's doorstep with two new goals in life that would be nearly impossible to accomplish. A real-life comparison of how difficult these goals were to achieve would be similar to climbing Mount Everest wearing only a light winter jacket. I had no clue how to accomplish either one of them. However, they both had something in common, which would provide a good starting point.

This place was the dark web. I started to understand this midway through this week of solitude. I thought that I needed to get into Erica's computer to retrace how she was led to something so evil.

By total coincidence, I happened to have Erica's computer with me, and after making some phone calls, I learned that Adam's father was a computer expert. I was thrilled when he agreed to assist me in searching for the information that I needed help to accomplish my new goals in life. Although he spent little time on the dark web recovering this information, the fee he charged to compensate for the legality of this recovery process was substantial. Luckily, I was able to borrow this money from Billy, no questions asked.

I made Adam's dad swear to tell no one about this, and then he explained to me just how illegal this was and that this made him a criminal... so common sense would naturally dictate the sanctity of our agreement. Regardless of how trustworthy this secret was, the last thing I wanted was for Erica to find out that I was snooping through her computer. I knew there was no way for me to explain that it was for a noble cause or that my reasoning was to avenge her sadness. This made me realize several things about my two new goals in life. The first was that it was obvious they were not normal goals for a person to have. Another would be the level of difficulty and how dangerous it would be to accomplish these goals. The last was that I couldn't tell anyone about them.

The spring winds blow the fall leaves into piles of nothing for summer to burn
Here we watch the ways of the righteous in hopes of being taught what they cannot learn
This is where my directionless journey was begun to find a deeper meaning of reason
In an effortless attempt to find myself within the inner-beauty of this season

Subconsciously walking through a forest of passion, I carved my name deep in a dying tree
I was left believing that it was meant to live but its soul was never set free
As the blue skies were being enlightened by the sun on this rather cloudy day
I wondered if true happiness were found, all my problems would be washed away

Not fully understanding itself, an answer was given in light of what it was thought to destine
Intentionally confused, the truth had lied to itself in spite of his own question
This created a harder problem to solve which led my mind to think a much deeper thought
Looking into my past, I learned from my mistakes a lesson that couldn't possibly be taught

As I finished carving my name, my motivation continued without knowing what to   intend
Now I was left wondering where I was and where this emotional journey would end.
Looking into the future, this dense forest ultimately left me with no path to follow
So I looked back at the tree and began to carve out a heart so deep I realized it was hallow

This revealed to me a memory of what had once lived within its empty existence
Before harsh conditions began weathering its growth, and ending its persistence Inspired
by the astonishing beauty contained in the life it was once living
True love began telling a story ending in the tragedy of a chance never given

To find something so amazing and understand something no one would ever know
I was left discontent with this world for never letting this tree continue to grow
Before I left this memory, true love deafened my hears as she cried out a name
Underneath this hollow heart I wrote the last letters hoping to end this pain

As I began to travel onward into the forest, the clouds began to weep
While the tree was left wreathing in the bitter cold as it fell into eternal sleep
Then an unexpected answer was given to explain a question with no conclusion
Incredibly confused, I turned around and saw God create the perfect illusion.

If a tree falls in a forest with no one around to hear... Does it make a sound?
I now knew the answer in the silence I heard as watched the tree fall through the ground
Standing there a man captivated by injustice, I couldn't believe my own eyes
Just as the truth has never found happiness believing the great sadness found in lies

Finally, I set forth into the forest of passion with new possibilities to endeavor
Continuing my journey to find the perfect tree that would grow forever

Chapter IX

Eventually, I decided to call Billy to see if he wanted to hang out. I really needed to get out of my bedroom. I decided to see if he wanted to trip on some of the acid I had brought back to Nebraska with me. In the back of my head, I figured I would also ask if he wanted to buy it all because I didn't want to have it anymore for a few personal reasons.

"Hey man, do you want to find something to do around this godforsaken town?" I asked, hopeful, sad, and confused about my life. "Honestly, I just need to get out of my house."

"Do you want to go fishing or something?" Billy asked.

"That sounds perfect."

"Okay, I'll grab some beer and pick you up in an hour… sound good?"

"I'll bring some acid with us too."

"Bullshit!" Billy responded. "You don't have acid."

"Yeah, I do. I brought some back from California."

"Holy shit, really? Then I'll be over in fifteen minutes," Billy said, with excitement in his voice.

"Sounds good, see you soon."

Once Billy picked me up, we got a case of beer and headed off to a small fishing hole a few miles outside of town on the Platte River.

After casting our lines out, we kicked back on some lawn chairs, with a beer cooler between us. Then, we decided to take two hits of acid each. It was a wonderful day to be fishing. The skies were clear, and the sun was shining. It wasn't too hot outside, and it wasn't too cold. It was excellent weather to inspire some fantastic psychedelic thoughts and a perfect day to go fishing.

"So, how was the West Coast?" Billy asked.

"It was cool, but not what I expected."

"Why is that?" This is when I told him about my entire trip, and Billy was pretty jealous.

"Are you back for good?" Billy asked.

"I don't know," I replied.

"Why did you come back?"

"I really don't want to get into it."

"Was it because of Erica?"

"Kind of, but kind of not," I said. "I just couldn't see myself living out there right now."

"But it was cool, though, huh?"

"Yeah, it was pretty cool. The ocean was awesome, and the cities were super cool to visit," I answered. "Have you ever been to California before?"

"No, but I want to go sometime," Billy responded.

"You got to see it," I said. "You should have come with me."

"Yeah, it would have been nice to get the fuck out of this town for a while."

"Do you think that you will ever move away from here?"

"Are you kidding me?" Billy said, with excitement in his voice. "Hell yeah, I do. I am moving away from Ogallala as soon as I save up enough money!"

"Don't you sell a ton of weed?" I asked, already knowing the answer. "You also own the biggest farm of anyone I know. According to my wallet, you are already rich."

"Yeah, I guess I have enough money to move if I wanted to," Billy replied.

"Then what is the problem?" I asked.

"Nothing, I just want to save more money... that's all."

"How much money do you have?"

"I don't know," Billy replied. "I have a few shoe boxes sitting around that I haven't counted yet, but it's at least a few hundred thousand dollars."

"You're shitting me!" I said, shocked with disbelief.

"I'm not kidding."

"Dude... where did you get all that cash?" I asked, trying to wrap my head around all this. "Did you make all that money selling weed to high school students?"

"Pretty much," he answered.

"You are lying!" I figured that if Billy were selling ounces for a hundred dollars a pop, he would have to sell about two hundred pounds of weed to make that kind of money.

"My harvest was huge last summer. It was almost three hundred pounds. People are coming from all over the state to buy it, too. I also lease over two thousand acres of my land to farmers who grow wheat and sunflowers."

"I had no idea you had so much money," I responded, still not completely believing him.

"Peanuts," Billy said, as he reeled in his hook. "I have planted over one thousand plants this year, which is five times what I planted last year. I have anklets catching leaves straight from Humboldt County, California. I invested five grand in seeds alone."

When I heard Billy explain his wealth, I thought of asking if he would help with some of Erica's dad's heart transplant expenses, but I stopped short. Instead, I asked, "Hey, dude, would you want to buy the rest of the three hundred hits of acid I have?"

"Fuck yeah, I would!" Billy said, as I watched him reel in his hook without a worm. "What do you plan on catching with that?"

"I'll catch something," Billy replied, reaching into his tackle box to grab another lure.

"So, do you even know where you would want to move to?"

"Yeah, I have it all figured out already," Billy said. "Well, unless you want to move somewhere cool with me."

"Like where?" I asked.

"I thought it would be awesome to attend college in Austin, Texas. I hear that the chicks down there are hot as hell, and they all party their asses off."

"Yeah, I don't think I'm cut out for college," I replied.

"Why not, man? Think of all the college parties. There would be so many babes getting drunk and wanting nothing more than Billy fucking, monkey lovin'. I would be hitting that shit all the time. A guy like me would be swimming in pussy. I think that college would be nothing but a good life! You should at least think about it."

"I can't move out of state to attend college," I explained. "And I don't think my folks can afford out-of-state tuition. Also, if you move to Texas to go to college, what will you do with your farm?"

"Sell it... or maybe give it to Adam or Eric," Billy said. "I plan to have so much money at the end of this year that it won't make any difference. I'll tell you what... I'll pay for your tuition if you come with me to Austin."

"I can't. Whatever my plans are, they need to include Erica," I said. "You know this."

"I thought she just dumped your ass," Billy replied.

"We're in love, dude. She will forgive me," I replied. "Besides, I know you're just kidding around."

"It's a good thing I came up with a plan B then," Billy said with an interesting smirk on his face. I could tell that the acid was starting to hit him partially because of his expression and also because I just felt it kick in myself.

"What's your plan B?" I asked.

"I'm going to move to Amsterdam next year!" he answered. "If you aren't coming with me, maybe I'll give my farm to you and Erica for a wedding present someday. I'm going to be your best man, right?"

"Yeah, I suppose so," I answered. "I haven't thought that far, but you are my best friend."

"You are my best friend too, Oliver," Billy said, just as his bobber sank. "Hey, did you see that shit?"

"Yep, I think you might have a bite," I responded.

"It's not doing anything now. I'll wait for him to really take it before I set the hook. I'll just sit here patiently and drink another beer. Do you want one?" he asked, holding out another beer. Then we both sat anxiously waiting for the bobber to sink again, but nothing happened.

"Dude, I think that fish took your bait."

"I suppose it wouldn't hurt to check it out," Billy replied.

"Hey," I said, "do you think we are having fun out here, or do you think this is boring?"

"What the fuck kind of question is that?" Billy asked.

"I mean, are we just out here killing time, or are we out here because this is what we want to be doing?"

"I still don't understand what you're trying to say," Billy said, with a puzzled look on his face.

"I guess what I am asking is... do you think we are doing what we should be doing? I don't have any real goals, and there sure as hell is nothing in Nebraska that inspires me to make any. It seems that most kids our age have got shit figured out. They know what they want out of their lives. I don't have a clue what I want to achieve with my life. I don't know shit! Do you know what you want to be doing in ten years, or for that matter, a year from now?" I asked.

"Shit yeah, you're just fucked in the head... that is all. I think that your girl has you pussy whipped, and she's probably filling your dome full of a bunch of bullshit. If you ask me... life is not overly complicated. You're born, you eat, shit, and die. It is as simple as that," Billy said, while baiting his hook again, this time with a worm. "There, if this slimy bastard doesn't look like a perfect dinner for a fish, I don't know what does."

"Good luck with that," I said. "But seriously, do you know what you want out of life?"

"Seriously, I do. I got shit figured out. No matter how old I get, I want to be doing the same thing that I am doing right now."

"What the fuck is that?" I asked, feeling puzzled.

"Smoking weed, drinking beer, and fucking every hot piece of ass that comes my way," Billy said, laughing and tripping balls.

"You know what job would be perfect for you?"

"What?" Billy asked.

"A manager for a strip joint in Las Vegas."

"Why is that?"

"Because you could party all of the time and hang out with naked chicks all day long."

"Naa, man, I ain't cut out for a nine-to-five job."

"You said you want to attend college... so what would you major in?" I asked.

"I probably wouldn't major in anything, but if I did, I would concentrate my studies on sexology," Billy explained.

"Sexology?"

"That's right, I want to study the fine art of banging bitches. I want to walk into class and get it on! Imagine having a hot-ass teacher teaching a lesson about sex. She would be all 'Look at my tits. These are some fine-looking titties," Billy said, gesturing a woman holding her breasts. "And this is a wet pussy. Now, I need a volunteer to come up here and fuck me!" That'd be a subject I'd want to study, and sign me up for the graduation ceremony. There would probably be a bunch of naked chicks on stage wanting to get banged. Sexology would be a degree I could handle... giving demonstrations on pussy-licking and fucking all day long... fuck yeah."

"It sounds like you got your work cut out for you," I replied.

"That isn't all... I have more plans," Billy said, while spitting some chew, drinking a beer, and smoking a cigarette.

"You're a fucking manic," I responded. "Okay... so what are these plans?"

"I plan to buy a used military aircraft carrier," he said, seeming completely serious.

"An aircraft carrier?" I asked, busting up with laughter. "And, I am sure these are sold for a dime a dozen."

"Shit yeah, think about it... the Bush administration... the fucking internet and shit."

"Good point," I added while shaking my head, "and what do you plan to do with an aircraft carrier? Invade third-world countries or something?"

"The first thing I'd do is go look for Gilligan's Island to rescue Mary Ann and Bunny. They are so fucking hot, and I bet that they're super horny too. Think about it... all they have is a house made of leaves, and I'd have an aircraft carrier," Billy said, staring off into space. "Mostly, I just want to pimp out an aircraft carrier."

I couldn't even begin to fathom what he was thinking at this point in the conversation because we were both tripping pretty hard. Still, I would have to admit that I was pretty interested in his plans to pimp out an aircraft carrier, so I asked, "How do you plan to pimp out an aircraft carrier... give it a paint job, install a sound system, and add a little tint to the windows?"

"For starters, yes, but first, my plan would begin by hiring a bunch of hookers. See, I intend to use my education to teach these hookers how to grow good weed and fuck my brains out! As I see it, anything is legal thirteen miles off the coast. So, I plan to install several grow rooms, a brewery, and a hard-core psychedelic drug lab in the basement!"

"I didn't know battleships had basements," I remarked.

"Aircraft carriers," Billy said.

"Whatever," I said, laughing. "You're such a dipshit."

"Shut the fuck up, smart ass, I'm going somewhere with this."

"Okay, carry on then..."

"So where was I... oh yeah, my aircraft carrier... anyway, on the ground level would be like combining the Red-Light District in Amsterdam with the Las Vegas strip. There would be nightclubs, casinos, strip joints, a McDonald's, and maybe a Seven-Eleven. On the next level, there would be hotel rooms, restaurants, and a hedge shop disguised as a police station, complete with a cop car sitting out front.... just to fuck with people, you know.

On the top level, I would have a driving range for golfers to launch golf balls into the ocean, as well as a football field, a basketball court, and a baseball field, no, wait... fuck the baseball field, a soccer field, no wait, better yet, a hockey rink, and a boxing ring... pool tables, ping pong tables, foosball tables, and... ah... ah... bowling lanes, and a big fucking pool and an even a bigger hot tub, and the biggest jukebox ever made, chalk full of tracks of Johnny Cash, Willie Nelson, and Hank Williams II... yeah... fuck yeah! And, the tower would have all the usual shit except for one thing."

"What's that? I asked.

"It would be operated by a bunch of Arabian suicide bombers standing beside a giant nuclear missile randomly aimed into the middle of nowhere... just to keep the world on its toes. Last but not least, I'd paint on the side of my ship, "Fuck your mom, world, I win!"

"You are nuts, man!" I responded, strangely perplexed by his concept of USS CRAZY FUCK. We were tripping on acid pretty hard at this point in time. I honestly didn't know if anything Billy had said to me all day had any truth. I didn't know if he had the money he talked about or if he actually wanted to move to Austin with me to go to college. I didn't know if he planned to move to Amsterdam or if there was any truth to wanting to give his farm to

Erica and me someday as a wedding present. Who knows, maybe he literally had intentions to buy a used aircraft carrier someday, for all I knew.

"I'll tell you what is fucking nuts," Billy replied. "We're sitting out here like dumbasses and not catching any fish. If we don't catch a fish here in the next twenty minutes... let's leave. Do you want to?"

"Sure," I answered.

We spent the rest of the day tripping nuts back at his farm after we quit fishing. This day was pretty awesome, considering how upset I was about my argument with Erica. Billy was a great guy to hang out with if you were feeling bad because he always had the dumbest shit to say. Judging by our conversation, you wouldn't know how intelligent and sincere he was, but in reality, he was one of the most genuine people I've ever known. In addition to that, he had farming figured out... and I mean dialed. It takes a pretty intelligent person to be a good farmer. Farming isn't easy, at least not if you plan to be successful, and Billy was successful.

Chapter X

A FEW DAYS LATER, I reunited with Billy and helped throw a party for Adam's birthday. Everything seemed to be set in place for a good party. Adam had just moved into his first apartment right around the time I left for California. One super cool thing about this apartment was that it had a giant courtyard with a swimming pool. It seemed to be the perfect place for a birthday party.

The word had begun to spread like wildfire about the party almost a week earlier, so there wasn't any question about whether there would be a good turnout. Billy bought us two kegs of imported micro-brewed beer from Colorado, a three-hundred-dollar handle of ten-year-old scotch, and four bottles of wine: a Sauvignon Blanc from Chile, a Cabernet Sauvignon from France, a Merlot from California, and a Chardonnay from Australia.

The party started about four o'clock in the afternoon. Immediately after the alcohol was put on ice, Billy and I gave cheers to Adam's birthday and decided to each take a shot. Then, we all cracked a beer, and the next thing we knew, we were getting pretty hammered. The first person to show up was Robyn, Adam's girlfriend. She would have been there since she woke up, but she had to work that day. There was rarely a time that Robyn and Adam were apart except when they were at work.

This was incredibly annoying. The worst part about it was when they would see each other after this short period of time. It was as if they had just spent years away from each other, stuck on separate deserted islands or something. They would make out anywhere... anytime, and this time was no exception. Robyn took a few shots right when she walked in the door, then, sure enough, she went right over to Adam's drunk ass and started to make out with him.

I remember shortly after Adam's apartment began to fill with people, we loaded up a bong that sat in the corner of the room, and began to smoke weed like a bunch of Rasta Farinas being treated in a Glaucoma hospital. After that, out came the LSD that I sold to Billy. I had no intention of tripping out that night, but I did smoke an awful lot of weed, which started to make me feel a little groggy. I remember looking around the room just before I passed out for an hour or so. Adam and Robyn were going back to Adam's room, most likely to have sex. Eric was sitting in front of the TV, and Billy was sitting across from me, about to trip balls.

I woke up probably about an hour and a half later to thirty people partying their asses off. I still had a burnt cigarette in my mouth and an empty can of beer in my hand. Unfortunately, I had spilled this can of beer all over my crotch. Either that, or I pissed my pants in my sleep, but I didn't have much time to think about it because I immediately felt the urge to puke. I noticed several people waiting in line when I looked over toward the bathroom. With little or no time to think about the situation any further, I ran outside and puked over the balcony, narrowly missing a couple of kids from our high school football team.

"Hey, watch it fucker," one kid yelled up to me.

"Yeah, learn how to handle your alcohol!" another kid yelled.

"Sorry," I responded.

"Are you all right, dude?" As I turned around, I saw this kid I knew from shop class holding three beers, and he didn't hesitate to hand me one.

"Thanks," I said.

When I walked back inside, I stood around for a few minutes, trying to find my friends. After walking back and forth a few times through the living room, dining room area, and kitchen, I didn't see anyone I was looking for. I figured Adam and Robyn would still be in his bedroom role-playing Adam and Eve, while Eric and Billy's whereabouts were probably somewhere tripping nuts in the apartment courtyard.

After refreshing my whiskey drink, I went down to the courtyard and eventually found Eric and Billy next to the pool, smoking a bowl with a few guys from the class below me. These kids that they were smoking with I would probably consider to be hillbillies, slightly different than rednecks, simply because they smoked weed.

I joined the circle next to Billy and began to listen to a conversation whirling around in a drunken frenzy. Once this bowl was smoked, a serious negotiation seemed to surface over an ounce of weed, but after twenty minutes of negotiation, two recently graduated topless cheerleaders suddenly began cheering from Adam's balcony. At this point, Billy just handed this guy the bag and said, "You wouldn't know a bag of weed if it hit you in the face. Have fun buying my weed and getting it from your friends with a middleman markup." Billy then turned toward me and said, "Let's go back inside to refresh our drinks and find out what is making those bitches so perky.

Things were really starting to get out of hand as the clock began to tiptoe toward midnight. Adam, who you would have thought to be monitoring the situation and enforcing a few house rules, was missing his entire birthday celebration. His apartment was now an absolute haven for teenage malevolence. Everywhere I looked, something was wrong, which included the fact that I had just been dealt a shitty hand out of a beer-soaked deck of cards.

I found myself playing a game of asshole, which I thought to be a clever name for a game designed to get you drunk. I was playing this game with a couple of popular people around town and a drunk girl sitting on my lap. The guy that sat to my right graduated with me and was a well-known wrestler in Nebraska. He had won the state championship in his junior and senior years in high school, which gave him a full-ride scholarship to KSU. This was a rather good thing, I guess if you were into wrestling. The guy that sat to his right was as famous of a person as we had in our town. He had won a bunch of eating contests and actually held some world records. This guy was fat, and when I say fat, I mean absolutely gigantic.

I'm not exactly sure who was determined to be the asshole of this game, but when the wrestler threw the table over, I quickly concluded that it was him. This caused the fat dude, who won the game of asshole, to throw the remaining contents of his cup at the jock. At this point, everyone in the room quickly came to a clear understanding with the saying, "Shit hit the fan!" as a glass actually hit the fan and chattered amongst a crowd of people.

Suddenly, everyone in the apartment stopped dead in their tracks and didn't say another word. It wasn't a huge apartment, so everybody's attention was focused entirely on the testosterone level of these two drunken bastards raising their fists. Fistfights were as much of a spectator sport as football or baseball in my hometown but were much more exciting to watch. Rarely did anybody ever step in to stop a fight, and nobody had any intentions of stopping this fight.

As the wrestler stood up from the table, he took off his shirt with jock-ridden rage, and it became noticeably clear to everyone that this kid was skinny... and I mean super skinny. As the fat kid stood up, it was obvious that he was fat... and I mean super fat. He was probably pushing four hundred pounds and was at least ten inches taller than the skinny kid. However, this considerable contrast in size didn't seem to discourage either one of them from walking head-first into each other's fists.

These two kids were exchanging some pretty harsh words as they began to make their way to the middle of the living room. Soon, everybody was cheering, and kids were already betting on the fight. I couldn't see how the skinny kid was going to get out of this alive. I mean, all the fat kid would have to do is sit on the jock and squish him to death. It would have been as simple as that.

The skinny kid landed the first blow with a right hook straight to the face. Dazed and confused, the fat kid surprisingly punched the jaw of the wrestler, which busted into a bloody mess... but this didn't end the fight. These kids were pissed off! Finally, with a remarkable attempt to take the fat kid down, the wrestler success-fully executed a pile drive. This caught everyone by surprise. It was something you would need to see to believe.

In any case, this really pissed off the fat kid, and he quickly broke free of the wrestler's headlock. That was when he began knocking over chairs and running around, flailing his arms about. Finally, in a full-on charge toward the skinning kid, the fat kid used all his weight and threw himself at the jock, taking down a shelf full of stereo equipment. CDs went flying everywhere, and the stereo itself fell onto the fat kid who was now crushing the hell out of the skinny kid.

At this point, Adam came out of his bedroom shouting, "What the fuck!" so loud the fat kid rolled over to see what was up, and "Bam!" Like a freight train on bad acid, Adam punched the fat ass squarely in the face. Blood squirted all over! There was no doubt that his nose was broken. He was out cold!

The wrestler tried his hardest to escape from under the fat kid, but he didn't get out in time. He got a hard kick to the head and then two punches to his face. Adam then proceeded to pull this scrawny kid out from under the fat kid by his arm and shirt. He picked him up, bouncer style, by grabbing him in a bear hug as he began manhandling him toward the door.

As Adam brought the wrestler outside, he grabbed the back of his pants and threw him down the concrete stairs leading up to his apartment. As Adam re-entered his apartment, he yelled at the top of his lungs, "Everybody, get the fuck out of here!" Dumbfounded by what had just happened, everybody just stared at Adam with blank looks on their faces, not moving, not blinking, not saying a word. "Now... mother fuckers!" Adam yelled again as he began to manhandle people out his front door.

Everybody got the point this time, and the room cleared very quickly. Before Adam closed the door on all of us, he asked Billy and me to help him get the fat kid outside. This kid was out cold, and you could see that his nose was broken badly. It took the combined efforts of all three of us to get him out of the door.

After the door to Adam's party was shut behind us, there were still a bunch of drunk kids in the courtyard finishing their beers and trying to decide where they would go. All of a sudden, the cops showed up, which caused everyone to scatter in all directions. Billy ran ahead of me and took off running down the street. I took off through the game room of the apartment complex and then through the laundry room, where, strangely enough, I found the girl who was sitting on my lap during the card game. I told her to come with me because the cops would most likely arrest her for underage drinking if they found her. After exiting through the back door of the apartment complex, we began cutting through people's yards and running down alleyways until we felt that we were a safe distance away from the cops.

"Holy shit," I said. "Did you see that?"

"What... the fight?" the girl asked.

"Yeah."

"No... I don't like watching fights."

"My friend Adam just kicked the shit out of those assholes I was playing cards with."

"You mean Mike and Ben?"

"I don't know... the skinny guy and the fat ass that sat beside him."

"Yep, that's Mike and Ben. They always get into fights. I just don't understand how they continue to be best friends."

"Fuck, fuck, fuck, Adam is going to be in so much trouble!"

We took a minute to catch our breath before I said, "Let's wait for a while and then go back down the street to see what's going on."

"Are you nuts?" she asked. "I'm not going back down there! We will get caught."

"No, we won't," I replied. "We will just wait awhile and check things out from a distance."

"Okay, that's cool."

After walking a block or two, I suddenly realized that I didn't know the name of this blond-haired girl I had been talking to all night and that we had never hung out before, "Do you even know who I am?"

"You're Oliver, right?" the girl responded. "You are friends with Billy and Eric... those guys, right?"

"Yeah," I responded, and just before I was going to ask what the girl's name was, my thought was interrupted by a couple of ambulances and even more police cars driving by. There were only a few mobile paramedics and nine police officers in our entire town. Looking down the street, I counted nearly all of them. Seven police cars, two ambulances, and a fire truck were in front of Adam's apartment. We could see lights flashing everywhere. The police were no longer concerned with drunk teenagers, and there was now a crowd of people from the apartment complex standing in the street, so I didn't feel afraid to stand amongst them.

After standing around for several minutes concerned about my friend, I watched the fat kid get carried out on a stretcher. It took six people to carry him. He must have been hurt pretty bad, I thought, because no one would put this much effort into carrying a person that large down three flights of stairs, through the courtyard, and across the street to the ambulance if there wasn't a good reason. The police officers and the fire truck stuck around at this point, but people started to go back inside the apartment soon after the ambulance sped off with the morbidly obese man inside. The blond-haired girl and I were also about to leave, but just before we did, we saw three police officers escort Adam out of his apartment in handcuffs.

"Adam is one of my best friends, and I'm really worried about what will happen to him," I told the girl as Adam was hauled away in the back seat of a police car. I sure hope that fat kid isn't injured too bad. He really got clocked, but his cheeks are so pudgy I thought they would have protected him from getting hurt no matter how hard Adam hit him... but I guess not.

"Yeah, no one would put that much effort into carrying that guy around if he wasn't hurt pretty bad. I bet he weighs five hundred pounds or more."

"That's the same thing I was thinking," I replied. "I suppose this would be a good time to go home. Where do you live?"

"Over on Tenth and Vine," the girl said. "It's right next to City Park."

"I live in that direction as well," I said. I was lying. I actually lived on the other side of town. I don't know if I was being a gentleman or if my intentions were douchebag related. "I'll just walk you home unless you drove your car to the party."

"I drove to the party, but I am not going back to get my car. It would be nice of you to walk me home," she replied, reaching for my hand. The only hand I ever held was Erica's. I was so distracted by this strange romance that I kept forgetting to ask the girl what her name was.

City Park was only a block from the girl's house and provided a shortcut to get there. This was a pretty big park, considering how small our town was. The park had a lot of trees along with tennis courts, basketball courts, and a big playground for kids. Everybody in our town made use of this park, particularly high school kids. My friends and I often came to this park to kick hacky sacks and toss Frisbees. There were always a bunch of jocks hanging out in the parking lot. I didn't like these people, but Billy sold them pot, so we smoked a lot of weed together. This parking lot was on the other side of the park from the girl's house, so I saw her and her boyfriend hanging out in his truck sometimes, but I never really paid any attention to them because they didn't smoke pot.

"Don't tell my boyfriend that I am doing this," the girl said, as we stopped in this parking lot under the street lights.

"Doing what?" I asked.

"This," she said, leaning toward me with a kiss. This was followed by more kissing as we walked into the park.

"Why is your boyfriend not here with you?" I asked.

"Troy went on a vacation with his family," she answered, wandering away from the streetlights. "Let's go this way."

"Troy, like the quarterback... Troy?" I asked as the name began to jog my memory. I suddenly realized that I had been making out with the girlfriend of the high school star quarterback. This was the same guy who I beat shit out of with his own helmet. His helmet had been sitting on a shelf in my parent's basement since my sophomore year in high school. I had a bad feeling I'd have to take it off the shelf if I continued to make out with his girlfriend.

"Yeah, that Troy," the girl replied.

"You probably shouldn't tell him we kissed each other," I said.

"Don't worry, I won't," she replied. "Besides, he is trying out for the Nebraska State football team this fall, and I still have another year left before I graduate from high school. This pretty much means that our relationship is coming to an end soon anyway. Actually, this would be as good a day as any to make it official. I guess I'll just have to tell him when he returns."

"Tell him what?" I asked, thinking I was missing something.

"That I'm breaking up with him," she replied.

"Okay, but you're still not going to tell him about us kissing... are you?"

"Not unless you want to get your ass kicked," she replied.

"Your boyfriend may get mad or angry, but that ain't going to happen," I answered.

"Yeah, right. He is about ten inches taller than you and can bench three hundred pounds," the blond-haired girl said. "How much can you bench?"

"It doesn't matter," I replied. "I was picked on a lot when I was a kid, especially by Troy. I hated him growing up. I remember your boyfriend sticking a firecracker up my ass and lighting my hair on fire when I was twelve. I got beat up three or four times a week until my first year in high school. Your boyfriend personally beat me up at least a dozen times, but he stopped wanting to fight me our sophomore year."

"Oh my God! Troy can be such an asshole. I'm glad he finally decided to quit beating you up."

"Yeah, me too," I said. "I'm glad nobody in this stupid town can beat me in a fight anymore. It doesn't matter how tall they are or how much they can bench press. The only way I'm ever going to get beat up again is if I got sucker punched or if the whole football team ganged up on me or something. Even then, it'd probably be a close fight."

"What makes you so strong?" she asked, while laughing at my comment.

"I'm not all that strong," I replied. "I'm just ridiculously good at fighting. I started boxing and learning karate the summer before my freshman year. I got pretty good at it by the tenth grade. Have you ever heard of someone called Jermain Taylor?"

"No," the girl answered. "Who's that?"

"The only guy I have lost a fight against since the summer before tenth grade."

"Does he go to our school?" the girl asked. "I have never heard that name before."

"No, he is from Little Rock, Arkansas," I answered. "Ask your boyfriend when he gets back what happened to his helmet during his sophomore year."

"Why should I ask him that?"

"Just ask him. He might even tell you about how good I am at fighting."

"Okay, I will. Then, I'll break up with him," she replied. "Or should I break up with him, and then ask about his helmet?"

"Does it really matter?" I asked.

"It probably doesn't."

"Do you think you are going to have sex with Troy again after you break up?" I asked.

"I'll probably have sex with him immediately after we break up," she said. "Why do you want to know?"

"Just curious, is all."

"Okay, and what about you? I thought that you were with that girl, Erica."

"We kind of broke up a couple of weeks ago," I replied.

"Oh, yeah, why?" she asked.

"I don't know… your guess is as good as mine," I responded with sadness.

"She broke up with you then?"

"Yeah, it kind of sucks," I said, looking at the ground.

"Oh, I'm sorry, Oliver," she responded. "Do you love her?"

"Yes," I answered.

"Yeah, I think that Troy and I are in love too, but I have to start getting used to the fact that he is leaving. I don't want to continue our relationship through my senior year in high school if he is going to be living across the state in Omaha. It would be impossible to be faithful to each other, considering how much we like to have sex," she said, giggling.

"What does Troy think about all this?"

"I have no clue, but he is really possessive over me. It sucks sometimes, but it will all work out. I'm sure everything between you and Erica will also work out."

"I hope so," I said.

"Until then, maybe we can hang out. That might help to cheer you up a little," the girl said.

"I don't think hanging out with you would be a good idea, especially if your boyfriend is possessive. He might find a bloody football helmet in the back of his truck if he got mad enough at me."

"I don't get it?"

"Inside joke," I replied. "I just don't think it'd be a good idea if we hung out together."

"Maybe we should just make the most of tonight then." We were lying on the grass in the middle of the park a few minutes later.

She really started to get hot when I unlatched her bra. It didn't take long for her shirt to come off and my pants to be unbuttoned.

"Should we be doing this?" I asked, thinking about the peculiar status of our current and recent relationships.

"Mmm...hmmm..." she responded while kissing my neck seductively. Then she pulled up my shirt and immediately went down on me with sensual kisses, slurping sounds, and an animal inclination to shamelessly suck me off. After pursuing the pleasures of the flesh with what had to have been one of the most stellar oral performances of her life, she rolled over onto her back and expected the sexual favor to be returned. I made a promise to the lord and myself that I'd lick her clit with unbridled enthusiasm for however long it took to make her pussy squirt and feel satisfied. Thankfully, my tongue understood its assignment and went muff diving with the perfect combination of effort and affection to quickly make good on my promises. I wanted to bring this girl to a screaming orgasm, and that is precisely how this erotic, cum-stained experience finally ended.

After several minutes of untamed passion and sexual exploration, our drunken libidos decided to stop just shy of having sex that night, as if this somehow meant that we were taking the moral high road back to our committed affairs. This experience simply intended to pleasure one another. It was a temporary escape from the obligations to our long-term relationships, which didn't seem like a lot for two horny teenagers to ask of the world.

At the time, I didn't understand what just happened or what I would come to understand as I continued my journey through life. My confused conscience and drunk mind had just been taught the definition of lust through an assortment of twisted thoughts and teenage sexual ambiguities. I never knew what lust felt like. This was because Erica was the only girl I had ever approached with sexual desire. Erica and I had been hopelessly in love since the day we met. No matter how horny or filthy our intentions were, Erica and I never experienced lust. The moral compass of true love does allow the heart to engage in capital vices or the seven cardinal sins. This doesn't mean that people in love are protected from the vanity of mankind. No one is immune to the expressions of pride, envy, gluttony, greed, lust, sloth, and wrath.

The park was dark enough that night to hide our naked bodies from the type of person that cannot keep a secret for the life of them, or just the random immoral intention of prying eyes. Unfortunately, it wasn't shady enough to keep the prying eye of my own conscience at bay. This experience inevitably left me with some odd misunderstandings about sex and my commitment to Erica.

As this night ended, the short distance between this sexual experience and the front steps of the blond-haired girl's house left no time to discuss what either one of us was thinking. Our awkward encounter finally ended with a kiss goodnight. I should have quickly forgotten this simple gesture because I was drunk. It meant nothing to either one of us, but it just made that night's sexual experience harder to understand. Unfortunately, this kiss goodnight was not what was on my mind when I sobered up enough to ponder the madness of love and the boundaries of infidelity.

Chapter XI

I DIDN'T HAVE ANY plans for the day after Adam's party other than watching some South Park episodes. I remember the phone ringing off the hook that morning. When I first woke up, I couldn't think of anyone I wanted to talk to, so I left it up to my parents to answer the phone. They must not have had anyone they wanted to talk to either because the phone never got answered the first few times it rang.

I spent part of the morning looking for a lighter and my lost remote control. I spent the rest of the morning in front of the TV with a gravity bong and a bowl of fruity pebbles, feeling pretty content with my few lazy plans for the day. After taking a few gravity bong hits, my attention was mostly focused on South Park characters. I couldn't figure out why Kenny had died and what Cartman was doing with a giant satellite sticking out of his ass. Unfortunately, the phone kept ringing several more times, interrupting my attempt to solve these cartoon enigmas.

Just as Chef began to explain his side of the story, the stupid phone started ringing again. By this time, I had become so annoyed that I just decided to answer the damn thing. The person who called wanted to tell me about credit cards. I spent about a minute listening to this guy's pitch before I finally interrupted him, "Holy shit, dude... shut the fuck up for a second!" I calmly said. "I think you want to talk to my father."

"Oh, I'm sorry," he replied. "Could I please speak with your father then?"

"If you know what's best for you, trust me... you would rather not."

"This concerns a new Visa Platinum credit card offer," he explained. "It is very important information. Can I please talk to your father?"

"I've listened to your bullshit offer long enough to know that my dad doesn't want it."

"Why is that?" he asked.

"My dad hates people, hates phones, hates credit card offers, and would really hate talking to you...that's why."

"This is something I would rather discuss with your father," he responded as if I were four years old.

"Listen, asshole... I'm way too stoned to walk all the way up the stairs just to piss off my dad. So, unless your bullshit credit card buys me a bag of weed, or offers a good explanation for the satellite sticking out of Cartman's ass, I'm hanging up this phone."

"Who's Cartman?"

"Exactly," I said, as I hung up the phone. Then, the phone immediately began to ring again. Thinking it was the credit card guy calling back, I answered, "Listen, mother fucker, I'm trying to watch South Park and finish my third bowl of Fruity Pebbles in peace. If you interrupt me one more goddamn time, I will crawl through this phone, wrap you in duct tape, and piss on your face! Then I'm going to send your stupid credit card offer on a one-way ticket straight up your ass!"

"Oliver?" The voice I heard instantly caused me to get a lump in my throat. I was at a loss for words. There was a suspenseful moment of silence, "Oliver, are you there?"

"Erica?"

"Yes, who did you think it was," she asked.

"I thought you were a guy from a credit card company that I had just hung up on."

"Good, I was hoping this wasn't how you answered the phone every time it rings."

"No," I responded. "This jackass was annoying the hell out of me, and you happened to call right at the wrong time."

"I can call back later," she replied.

"Oh no, Erica, there is never a wrong time to talk to you."

"That's sweet to say... so what's up?"

"Nothing, really. I wasn't expecting to get a call from you," I said.

"I hadn't spoken with you for a while, so I thought I would give you a call."

"Right on! What have you been up to?" I asked. "Is your father doing better?"

"Yeah, he is home now and doing much better."

"That's good to hear," I said.

"How have you been?" I asked. "I didn't see you at Adam's party last night. How come you didn't go?"

"I just didn't feel up to it. Sherly came with me to go see Scary Movie 2 instead," Erica replied, "but I heard all about the party."

"Oh yeah... what did you hear?"

"I heard it was pretty crazy."

"Yeah, it was nuts!" I replied. "Adam ended up beating the shit out of a couple of kids for breaking his stereo, and then he got arrested."

"Ya, I know," Erica replied.

"What did you hear?" I asked, more interested in who she talked to than what she heard. "And who did you hear it from?"

"Sherly's dad was one of the paramedics that responded to the call," Erica explained. "He couldn't say much about it because there is a big investigation going on, but I guarantee that it will be on the front page of the newspaper today and on the six-o-clock news tonight."

"I doubt it is in today's paper because his party was busted after midnight."

"That's true," Erica said, taking a moment to breathe. "You know what, Oliver?"

"What's that?"

"I didn't call you to talk about Adam's party," Erica said with an emotional tone. "I called you to apologize."

"For what?" I asked, instantly accepting her apology and anything she planned to apologize for.

"For being such a bitch to you when you came to see me after returning home from the west coast. You had every reason to be upset. I thought a lot about it before coming to the realization that what you said was taken out of context, and you don't actually think I was a slut."

"Yeah, of course, I don't think you are a slut. You're the exact opposite. It's me that should apologize for losing my shit and not telling you the truth about why I came back home," I responded. Even at an early age, I understood that an apology from a woman in her position was unusual and needed to be reciprocated carefully and sincerely. I knew that what I just said was only a summary of my apology. I would need to be more thorough and express my sincerity as our conversation continued.

"What do you mean?"

"About what?" I asked.

"About coming back home?"

"I came back home because... shit... hold on a second... there is someone on the other line."

(click)

"Hello," I answered.

"Yo dude, what up?" I heard Billy say.

"Nothing much," I responded, "Hey, can I call you back? I have Erica on the other line."

"Sure, but call me right back!" Billy said, with concern in his voice "It's about Adam... he killed that fat dude who busted his stereo!"

"No fucking way!"

"Serious!"

"Holy shit! Okay, I'll call you right back... no, wait... just stay on the phone," I said.

(click)

"Erica... Are you still there?"

"Yeah, what's up?"

"That was Billy," I frantically replied. "You are not going to believe this."

"What happened?" Erica asked.

"He told me that Adam accidentally killed someone who came to his party last night," I quickly explained. "So, I got to take this call."

"No way... are you serious?" Erica asked. "You're just fucking with me, right?"

"Not unless Billy is fucking with me," I answered, concerned as hell.

"Okay, but call me right back," Erica responded.

"I will."

(click)

"Billy... are you still there?"

"Yeah... I'm still here," Billy replied.

"What the fuck happened?"

"Apparently, that fat guy was dead by the time the paramedics arrived, and now Adam is being charged with murder!"

"HOLY SHIT!" I yelled. "What's going to happen to him?"

"I have no clue," Billy answered. "This is so fucked up!"

"Who did you hear this from?"

"I just got off the phone with his mom!" Billy explained. "She was all crying and shit.. asking me what happened?"

"What did you say?"

"I didn't say shit!"

"This is fucking nuts!"

"Fuck yeah, but dude, I got to let you go," Billy frantically said, "That's Eric on the other line."

"Okay, but if you find out anything else... call me!"

"I will... late."

(Ring...ring...ring)

"Hello?" Erica answered

"Adam is in jail for murder!"

"Oh my God! This can't be happening," Erica replied.

"I shit you not!"

"Wow!" Erica responded. "I don't even know what to say."

"I hope Adam figures out how to get out of all this. It's not like he meant to hurt anyone. He was just mad that his stereo was broken," I replied, preceding a long, difficult pause in our conversation. We sat in this eerie silence for several minutes, trying to wrap our heads around the situation and the horrific news that we had just heard about our friend. I finally broke this silence by saying, "This has been the most emotional week of my life!"

"Yeah, this is really, really fucked up," Erica stated.

"I'm not talking about Adam," I replied. "I'm mostly talking about you. I have felt so lonely and sad since last we spoke. My chest hurt all week. It felt like my heart was broken."

"I'm sorry, Oliver."

"But then you called, and I was so happy. When I heard your sweet, beautiful voice... I just melted. I love you so much, Erica. You have no idea how much you mean to me," I emotionally explained. "It really sucked hard when Billy called and told me about Adam, and this news is making me feel so super shitty. Do you know what's ironic about all this?"

"What's that?" Erica asked.

"Talking to you makes me incredibly happy, but this news about Adam makes me incredibly sad, and it feels weird," I explained. "I have so much I want to say to you, but I don't know if I will sound happy or sad when I talk to you."

"You can sound any way you want, Oliver," Erica replied. "I just want to know the truth about why you came back home and what your plans for the future are. Do your plans include me?"

"Honestly, I went out to California super excited about everything and didn't know what to do when I got there. I went to a couple of cool places, I guess, and I wanted to trip on LSD for the first time. So, I traveled around searching for people who looked like they were tripping, and I eventually bought some acid from a guy I met in Venice Beach. His name is Fredrick, and he is a super cool, hardcore hippy. This guy is an awesome person! He let me stay on his couch for a week and then he drove us up to a Phish concert in Colombia River Gorge. This trip was crazy! I'll tell you all about it at a different time. Anyway, when we returned to Venice Beach, I suddenly realized that I couldn't live without you," I explained with an emotional tone. "So, I just decided to come back home."

"Whoa," she said. "Back up... so you ate acid?"

"Yeah," it was pretty awesome."

"That is crazy! I was told by our history teacher, Mr. Singleton, that you are officially insane for life if you eat acid. Do you feel insane now?" Erica asked, completely serious... like dead ass serious. Erica always asked me questions like this. Sometimes, I thought it was annoying how oblivious she was to common sense questions, but I mostly found this to be absolutely adorable. If you sat around listening to Erica talk, you might think she was a bit dim-witted. For example... someone asked her who the president was shortly after George Bush Jr. was elected, and she didn't know who the president was. The thing is... Erica is pretty damn smart, maybe not in a way that she understands who the president of the United States is, but intelligent in ways that make sense to her. The bottom line was that she didn't waste any time thinking about things that didn't matter to her... and I guess she didn't care about who the president was.

"Oh my God!" I responded. "Tripping on acid did not cause me to go insane. It just wore off, and then I felt normal again."

"What was it like?" Erica asked, in a voice that sounded like I had just found E.T. in my bedroom closet.

"You just think about some amazing things, hallucinate a little, and laugh a lot."

"Whoa," she said. "That's crazy! What did you see when you hallucinated? Did you see ghosts?"

"No, I didn't see any ghosts," I replied with a giggle, "I mostly just saw weird shapes and colors."

"Whoa," she said. That is crazy! What did the shapes and colors look like?"

"I can't remember because they were hallucinations."

"Whoa," she said. That is crazy!"

"I brought a few hits back from California just in case you ever wanted to try it."

"I doubt I will," Erica replied. "I'm not sure if I'd like to see weird shapes and colors."

"It also makes things super funny," I replied. "You laugh at all sorts of crazy stuff."

"Like when you smoke pot?"

"Ya, sort of, but it's just different," I explained. "You should try it."

"I need to figure out what is going on with my dad first... then maybe."

"I understand," I replied. "Speaking of which, I didn't do any-thing to your computer. It's just sitting in my room. You can have it back whenever you want."

"Awesome! I was afraid to ask for it back," Erica explained with excitement in her voice. "I thought you might have thrown it in the garbage. I cannot afford to buy another computer, so I was hoping you didn't destroy it, but I would have understood if you had."

"I would never destroy anything of yours. I was just furious the other day and didn't want some creepy man to be looking at you naked."

"Are you still mad at me about that stuff?"

"I'm not mad at you," I answered, thinking about how delicate her feelings were and how naive she was about the situation. "It worries me because he could have been recording you and selling the videos online."

"I don't think he did that," she replied, completely unsuspect-ing of how evil this person was. "Do you think he was recording me?"

"No," I answered, knowing nearly for a fact that he was, but I didn't want to make Erica feel any worse about all this than she already did.

"Yeah, I think he was just a gross, old pervert that sells informa-tion about heart transplants, and since I couldn't pay him..."

"Erica, stop!" I demanded. "I don't want to know anymore, okay? Just promise me that if I give back your computer, you will never contact that person again."

"I promise," she answered, "but an illegal heart transplant is the most realistic way of saving my dad's life."

"Erica, just save as much money as you can. I discovered that Billy has way more money than I thought and sells way more weed than I thought. I have discussed a plan to get you this money, but it will take some time." I felt bad about telling her this because I knew that even if I did discuss this with Billy, no plan of ours could come up with over a million dollars. However, I was confident that I would figure out something to get this money. I just didn't have any good ideas yet.

"Really? Oh my God! That would be so awesome!" Erica excitedly replied. "Because the can with my dad's picture on it at the supermarket hasn't even raised a thousand dollars yet."

"Yes, really." After this conversation and a few others, I realized that Erica didn't understand how much money a million dollars was. "And, just let me handle the black-market stuff if we have to go that route, okay?"

"Okay," she answered. "Now, will you tell me why you came back home?"

"I thought that I told you already," I responded.

"You said that you missed me, but you didn't tell me exactly why you decided to come back home."

"The reason why I left this town in the first place is because I hate this goddamned town and most of the people that live here, but I would hate my life if I didn't get to spend it with you. I love you more than anyone, anything, and any place in this entire world. The truth is that I don't want to live in this stupid town forever, but it would be impossible to live anywhere without you. Everywhere I go in this world, I want you to be there with me... and everywhere you go in this world, I want to be there with you. If you want to know the truth about why I returned home, it was because you weren't with me. You were here in Ogallala, so I came back home to be with you. You will always be included no matter what my plans are for the future. My only plans right now are to love you and to make you happy."

"Oh my God!" Erica replied, sniffling with happy tears, " Oliver, that is the most romantic thing you have ever said to me! I love you so much!"

"I love you too."

"Can you guess what I am thinking right now?"

"Ummm... no... what are you thinking about?"

"I'm coming over to give you the best blowjob of your life! Get naked. I'll see you in two minutes... maybe less!"

Chapter XII

The following week was pretty interesting. The elephant in the room was that I had sex, or almost had sex with a blond-haired girl, which carried a heavy burden. I talked with Erica about our break, but it was never determined if we were actually broken up. Regardless of whether I was technically cheating on Erica or not, it still felt like I had compromised an element of purity in our relationship. Nevertheless, everything seemed to be headed in the right direction between Erica and me for now.

As hard as it was on my conscience to think about what happened in the park with the blond-haired girl, the reality of Adam's incarceration was substantially worse to think about. He was being held on a fifty thousand dollar bond, and no one could come up with this sort of cash. His parents called me at least a couple of times a day, trying to get information about this accident. To make matters much worse, his girlfriend, Robyn, was utterly hysterical and attempted suicide two days after Adam was charged with murder. Her parents found her foaming at the mouth in their bathroom after swallowing an entire bottle of pills. After the ambulance came and she got her stomach pumped, she ended up suffering a horrible stroke and lost feeling in the entire right side of her body. Robyn never recovered. After years of rehabilitation, she still is not able to walk or move her right arm.

Erica and I went to visit Adam's girlfriend in the hospital right before going to the funeral for the kid whom Adam allegedly murdered. This funeral was one of the strangest things I had ever seen happen in our town. I could not believe it! It seemed as if the entire city shut down for the afternoon so people could attend the funeral. At least a thousand people, reporters, and news vans from around the state showed up.

However, it wasn't the crowd of people that attended that made this funeral so odd. The open-casket reception ceremony before the funeral was likely immoral in the eyes of God, but it was just a bizarre experience for the people attending this reception. A single-file line was formed, stretching all the way around the block surrounding the city morgue. I couldn't believe how many people wanted to pay their respects to this morbidly obese man. Erica and I stood in that line with my pals for over two hours before finally realizing how strange this funeral was. I thought it was a little weird before I even saw the casket, but my mind was blown at this point.

The fact that this incredible person had an enormous casket was just one of many unusual things about the funeral reception. As gigantic as the casket was, there was no way all the shit that people brought to be buried with the morbidly obese man was going into the grave with him. The hole would have had to be forty feet deep to fit all this junk. To make matters worse, there was a lady standing next to the deceased man who seemed to be in charge of what made it into the casket. From my perspective, it appeared that anything this woman could sell at a rummage sale never made it in the casket and was being piled into the corner of the funeral home. The things in this pile created the most obscure collection of random things that I had ever seen in my whole life!

What I could see sticking out of the pile were hundreds of action figures. There were GI Joe, Masters of the Universe, and Teenage Mutant Ninja Turtles. I also saw Elf, the Incredible Hulk, and Mr. T. I saw at least fifty Beanie Babies and every Barbie doll that was likely ever made. There was a stack of Neil Diamond records, several cases of beer, and from what I was told, every Newsweek and National Geographic Magazine printed since 1989. There were pizza boxes still full of pizza, a pogo stick, six milk crates full of science fiction and romance novels, a dart board, a tackle box, and the entire series of both, the Planet of the Apes and Conan the Barbarian. The list goes on and on...

The most impressive thing I saw at the ceremony was a five-foot high trophy for winning the world championship hotdog eating competition. This was the tallest trophy sitting amongst the pile of shit that wasn't going to make it into the morbidly obese man's casket, but it was far from the only trophy. This man apparently won hundreds of eating contests and had the trophies to prove it. I didn't know this before the funeral because I didn't ever watch the news or pay attention to current events, but this morbidly obese man held a number of world records. If you look up eating competitions in the Guinness Book of World Records, you'll find a picture of this man holding a hotdog.

With this said, the things that made it into the casket were also pretty strange. The three things that I specifically noticed were the beer mug this guy was holding the night he died and a big yellow pair of worn-out slippers with Donkey Kong's head on the front... one of which appeared to have been chewed up by a dog. There was also a big pile of Beatles memorabilia, which was likely the only items that made it in the coffin worth any money, but the woman deciding what made it in the casket didn't seem to be the type of person who enjoyed listening to music, so it kind of made sense.

I stood there looking at this woman standing between the morbidly obese man's coffin and the pile of shit stacked in the corner. After watching this bizarre ceremony for nearly twenty minutes, I thought that more things should be going in the casket. This bothered the hell out of me for some reason, and the longer I stood around, the more troubled I became. I eventually approached this lady and said, "Hey, what the hell is happening here? Apparently, this guy had a lot of friends, who all want to put their weird shit in his coffin. Who are you to say what goes in his grave and what stays out?

"I'm his mother," the lady replied. "Who the hell are you?"

I stood there looking at this angry woman with a perplexed thought in my head for only a second before I was suddenly pushed out of the way by someone who had just brought in a keg of beer. I couldn't believe what I was looking at! This keg of beer sat in the corner of the morgue for only a couple minutes until somebody else in line walked up with a beer tap. Incidentally, this caused the morbidly obese man's mother to start yelling the most noble thing I had heard her say throughout the entire funeral ceremony, "Hey, does this look like a party to you?" I gained a little more respect for the morbidly obese man's mother after she said this, but I'm still confused about what difference it made to her when she stood beside the casket with a tallboy Pabst Blue Ribbon in one hand and a menthol Virginia Slim cigarette in the other.

I was one of about fifty people in the funeral home who looked at this woman with a blank expression. I didn't even want to know what would happen if someone answered her question, so I grabbed Erica by her hand and ran for the door. Erica and I skipped the burial altogether because we both felt that we had seen enough for one day. I felt terrible about all this. It was incredibly sad that this man died, and it made me feel worse that Adam was responsible for his death. This guy was a local celebrity who will go down in history as a legend. This was the most popular person in town and the only famous person who had ever lived in Ogallala. Over two decades later, a picture of this guy holding a hot dog is still hanging on the walls of nearly every restaurant in town.

Later that evening, Erica and I were watching a movie at my house when the phone began to ring. Sherly called to ask us if we wanted to go to a party with her. Apparently, this party was organized to celebrate the life of this kid whose funeral we had attended earlier in the day. Erica agreed to go and asked me if I wanted to come with her. Considering my involvement in the matter, I thought it would have been appropriate for me to attend, so I called Billy to see if he was going, and he felt the same way about the situation. Afterwards, I called Eric, and he wanted to go as well, so I guess the whole gang was going except for Adam.

I had a gut feeling that something would go wrong that night before I even left my house. I just wished Erica and I had continued watching movies rather than attending this stupid party. The plan was for Erica to run home to change and adjust her makeup. Then, Sherly would swing by to pick her up before coming to my house to pick me up. As much as I didn't want to go to this party, I needed to make some personal hygiene adjustments before I went: shower, shave, brush my teeth, and change clothes.

Right about the time Sherly was supposed to swing by, two Jehovah's Witnesses came to our door. My mother must have answered the door because my dad would have probably just slammed it shut on them. In any case, I had just walked up the stairs when I heard my father say, "Honey, just let me handle this." After listening to a brief description of their religion, my father calmly said, "You know, that sounds pretty interesting, but how can I trust you?"

"What do you mean?" the witness asked.

"Well, here let me show you what I think you are trying to tell me, and you just let me know whether my family and I would be right for your religion," my dad responded,

"Okay," the man replied, looking a little confused. "What do you want to show us?"

"Well, I'll tell you what... give me your shoes along with your socks, and I will demonstrate." Despite his bewilderment about what my father planned to do with his shoes and socks, the man didn't ask any more questions. He just took them off and handed them to my father. My mother and I knew better and could only imagine what my father planned to do next. I was finding it incredibly hard to keep a straight face as this naive man handed over his shoes and socks, as my father requested.

My father then placed this man's shoes and socks on the table and unbuckled his pants just before he turned around, exposing his bare ass to the Jehovah's Witnesses. Completely appalled and utterly disgusted by my dad's ass, neither one of them knew how to react as my dad grabbed one of the shoes off the table and proceeded to take a shit in it.

My mother yelled, "Oh my God, you are not doing that right here in our living room!" Covering her mouth with abhorrence, she walked into the kitchen, shaking her head. I thought that this was funny as hell, and so I started laughing my ass off just as my dad grabbed the other shoe off the table and shit in it as well.

Once my dad was finished with his shit, he handed back this guy's shoes, and the Jehovah's Witness actually grabbed them back from my dad. This was when my dad grabbed his socks off the table and used them to wipe his ass, and he handed this back as well. This whole time, my mom was yelling at my dad, saying things like, "Oh my God, Jim, that is so gross!" All this yelling and commotion caused my sisters to come to see what was going on as well, and so they also started to chime in, "Dad is so disgusting!"

I laughed so hard at the man's terrified expression while holding his shit-filled shoes that I could barely breathe. At this point, I remember myself rolling on the floor with laughter, trying my best not to puke. Then, just as my father opened up the door to kick the two Jehovah's Witnesses out of our house, by unfortunate coincidence, Erica and Sherly showed up on my doorstep. I didn't say a word as I walked out the front door. I just walked right passed the poor guy holding his shitty socks and shoes and left for the party. Both Erica and Sherly had a look of horror on their faces while trying their best to make sense of the situation. I simply responded, "You don't want to know."

Chapter XIII

When we finally arrived at the party to celebrate the morbidly obese man's life, I noticed that the same keg of beer brought to the funeral earlier that day was sitting in the host's backyard. Erica, Sherly, and I had just filled up our glasses when we saw Billy and Eric walking up to us. Then, the four of us stood around for several minutes, discussing how strange the funeral was and how awkward it was to attend this party.

It didn't seem as if anyone noticed or cared that Billy and I had helped to carry this guy out of Adam's apartment. Feeling pretty confident that the situation couldn't get any more awkward than it already was, I decided to make the most out of the party. Oddly enough, I found myself somewhat enjoying the party right up until I saw the blond-haired girl with who I almost had sex in the park.

She was standing next to her boyfriend, Troy, who was pumping the tap on the keg. I quickly turned around when I saw her, hoping she wouldn't notice me. I had not told anybody about what had happened between us, and with all the bullshit that had occurred over the last few days, I had managed to put our sexual encounter in the back of my head, clear of obsession for the most part.

When I turned around, I saw Sherly and Erica standing behind me. Then, I looked over to see Billy and Eric passing a joint back and forth to each other about twenty feet away, but I just stood there, not wanting to participate in the conversation about Adam or smoke a joint with my pals. I was more concerned about encountering the blond-haired girl and her possessive boyfriend. The gut feeling I had earlier in the night that something was wrong had now turned into a full-blown panic attack.

At this point, I began searching for a good excuse to leave, so I started telling the gang that I was feeling sick and thought the keg might have some bad beer in it. I asked them if someone wanted to leave the party and find something else to do, but there really wasn't anywhere to go. Around this time, I remember looking over my shoulder and seeing that my worst nightmare was about to come true when I noticed the blond-haired girl and her boyfriend walking toward me.

Hoping to dodge this awkward encounter, I asked the gang if someone could give me a ride back home. Unfortunately, I didn't get a response in time. When I turned around to see if they were still walking toward me, I found them standing right behind me. I was pretty freaked out by this situation because of the infidelity issue and because Troy looked super pissed off, which caused me to think that he likely knew what had happened between his girlfriend and me.

"Is there anything you would like to say to me?" Troy asked, taking another step toward me, getting right in my face.

"No, I can't think of a damned thing except that your breath smells like shit," I replied, while taking a step back.

"I thought that you might want to tell me about how you fucked my girlfriend?" Troy said, as he took another step toward me. His crossed brow, red face, and heavy breathing through his nose were cause for concern at this point because his football helmet was sitting on a shelf in my parents' basement.

"I don't think so," I responded, intentionally trying to sound confused. "What is your girlfriend's name?"

"Tracy Coffman."

"No, I can't say that I have fucked any girlfriends named Tracy Coffman lately, but if I do, I'll be sure to let you know." When I said this, he suddenly took a step backward with a creepy smile on his face. It was obvious that he was just about to go against his better judgment and attempt to punch me. However, it took him a few seconds to think about it. That is when I said, "Are you sure you want to do this, buddy? We both know how this is going to end."

"Everyone knows you haven't been in a fistfight in almost two years. I bet you probably forgot how to punch someone without boxing gloves on... you fucking pussy."

"It's possible," I replied, "but do you really want to fuck around and find out? Why don't you consult with some of your football buddies before you potentially make a life-altering mistake."

By now, a crowd of people were standing around watching us, and some of them really wanted to see us fight. It would be unusual for there to be a party without someone getting their ass kicked, so I felt that it may as well be this guy. Conversely, most people at this party were also at Adam's party not long ago. The fact that someone died at that party provided plenty of reasons for us to back off and wait to resolve our differences at a different time. Unfortunately, this was not how it would go down as I soon found myself in the middle of a small circle of recently graduated high school kids chanting, "Fight, fight, fight!"

It was no surprise to see a handful of Troy's teammates at this party, and two of them wanted revenge for losing some fights with me during our sophomore year. As I looked around, I realized I was about to get jumped. Troy initially came at me with a haymaker, but I countered this by punching his stomach and elbowing him in the back of his head. Two of his friends came at me at the same time, and one of them was almost able to land a solid blow. His missed opportunity for hitting me in the face with an unethical victory punch was countered with a single punch that knocked him out cold. Troy was still recovering from getting the wind knocked out of him, so I thought this left me with a one-on-one matchup with one of his other teammates. It didn't end well for him either, as I quickly laid him out with a single punch as well. A strange coincidence occurred when the second football player I knocked out landed directly on top of the first.

With a small pile of football players already lying on the floor, knocked out and bloody, I thought this left only Troy to deal with, and that was if he dared to keep fighting. Unfortunately, I was wrong about this assumption. While watching Troy stand back up with no self-esteem and little chance of winning this fight, I suddenly felt someone from the crowd randomly hit me in the back of the head. I quickly learned at this point that the fight wasn't a guaranteed victory when I turned around to see who had hit me. In addition to the cheap shot artist who hit me in the head, there were six more of Troy's teammates standing there with angry looks on their faces. These guys were obviously not on my side, but they were not exactly looking for a fight either.

This was when I turned back to see where Troy was at and to finish this brawl. Unfortunately for me, when my back was turned, he was unsuspectingly preparing a second attempt at landing a hay-maker, which was surprisingly executed to perfection. This punch hit my face like a heavy brick and knocked me to the ground. Then he started kicking my ribs and the back of my head. He ended up knocking me the fuck out at some point with one of several kicks to the back of my head. Thinking back on this situation, I probably deserved it at least a little bit, and I am glad it was him who knocked me out rather than one of his friends. Even though I was far from the biggest problem facing his relationship, I hope he felt a little vindicated after this.

Erica and my friends were in the crowd of spectators when I got knocked out. I laid there, face down in a puddle of water, unconscious for the next several minutes. During this time, Billy and Eric began beating the shit out of Troy. Billy was a great fighter but probably didn't contribute much to the fight because Eric was a scrapper with raw talent. When I finally came to, I found myself in the middle of a crowd of teenagers settling their bets on this brawl.

I continued to lie on the ground for a few minutes, paralyzed from the pain in my head while adjusting to reality after spending nearly a half hour completely unconscious. I didn't expect anyone to feel sorry for me, but I figured there would be at least someone to help me up. When I finally collected myself enough to stand up and get my sorry ass out of the puddle of mud, I saw Billy rolling a blunt on the hood of a car parked near the garage. I also saw Erica and Sherly through a crowd of people standing several feet away with their backs turned.

"Hey, Billy, what happened?" I asked after taking a short walk toward the garage.

"First of all, you got punched in the face and looked like a fucking pussy when you fell into that puddle over there. Eric and I really didn't feel sorry for you, but we kicked that football player's ass anyway. We had to beat down a few more of his teammates as well. Then, some drunk cheerleader jumped in to try to save the day by breaking up the fight, but the fight was already over by that point."

"Thanks, I appreciate you guys getting revenge on those assholes for sucker-punching me."

"You are welcome, but unfortunately for you, after that asshole got the shit kicked out of him, he stood back up and began to rant and rave about you fucking his girlfriend in the park. I got to tell you, Oliver, this guy sounded pretty convincing. If I weren't certain that you were born without balls enough to admit you have no dick, I would have believed this guy. Considering how hot that girl was, I bet most any guy would have fucked her had they been given the opportunity. Hell, I might have even tried to hit it if I were younger and standing in your shoes."

"You are kidding me, right?"

"No, really, I might have hit it, and I truly believe that you have no dick," Billy said sarcastically.

"Seriously, what did Troy say?"

"Who's Troy," Billy asked.

"The football player that you just beat up. Who the hell do you think I'm talking about?"

"Settle down, buddy... how the hell am I supposed to know what his name is? Anyway, he just kept going on and on, yelling out all sorts of crazy shit about how you fucked his girlfriend in the city park the other night."

"What happened to him?" I asked. "Where did he go?"

"I don't know… I guess he must have run away after figuring out how much of a brute Eric was.

"What happened to the guy that broke up the fight?"

"Well, Eric punched him in the stomach, and that was when all sorts of kids started to gang up on Eric."

"What were you doing at this point," I asked.

"I was laughing at your sorry ass lying in the puddle of mud over there."

"What happened to Eric?"

"He ended up taking down two more guys before the fight suddenly stopped."

"Why did it stop?" I asked.

"I don't know… Eric probably got tired of kicking the shit out of people, I guess. You should have seen the rest of this brawl because Eric was a total badass. I got to tell you Oliver, I think you and Eric might be a pretty fair fight.

"So, where is Eric now?"

"What is this… the one hundred and one questions it takes before you admit you're a pussy? How the hell am I supposed to know? If I were him, I would be fucking that stupid football player's girlfriend because I didn't see her leave with him… and she was looking pretty hot tonight. I also heard that she is pretty easy and likes to fuck in the park, so the only thing that I could see holding him back would be that she'd be sloppy seconds to your drunk ass."

"Fuck you! Billy."

"Hey man, don't shoot the messenger… and instead of getting all upset with me, you should probably be figuring out what you're gonna say to Erica. You are in trouble, dude. She's pissed… really pissed!"

After talking with Billy, I walked around the party feeling pretty disoriented. This was likely caused by a combination of things, including smoking a blunt with Billy, getting knocked out by Troy, my unknown future with Erica, and the anxiety caused by this entire situation. I tried to think of what I could say to Erica to alleviate the circumstances, but I didn't come up with anything before she found me.

"Oliver, are you alright?" Erica asked, genuinely concerned. I tried to avoid her question by acting too disoriented to answer. I just stared at the ground and held my head while making low-pitched sounds of pain. Unfortunately, Erica continued to ask me questions. When I finally looked up, undoubtedly with an expression of guilt, I could barely look into her eyes. She figured out that something was wrong at this point. I could blame my rotten demeanor on trying to recover from getting knocked out, but I knew it was only a matter of time before she began asking questions I didn't want to answer.

As I anticipated, she eventually started to sound upset with me and finally yelled, "Oliver, stop playing stupid...what the hell was that all about?" This question was asked with a threatening tone in her voice, which I interpreted to be the straw that broke the camel's back. If I hadn't started to come up with answers at this point, the situation would have only gotten worse.

"I don't know?" I responded, once again trying to disarm and deflect further inquiries.

"Bullshit!" she said. "Some guy is not going to pick you out of the woodwork and want to beat the shit out of you for no reason at all. Plus, he certainly wouldn't be blaming you for fucking his girlfriend if he didn't have a pretty good reason to think that you did."

"Maybe he had mixed me up with someone else," I answered.

"Oliver, his girlfriend, was standing right behind him, and I can tell that you are lying by the look on your face. Is it true... did you fuck his girlfriend?"

"Well, you had broken up with me, and I was drunk, so..."

"So what?" Erica interrupted.

"I don't know," I answered as I began to understand the gravity of my mistake. This may have been one situation in which it probably would have been better to have just flat-out lied or at least found a better way of avoiding the truth. However, that likely would have created an even bigger problem to deal with at some point in our relationship.

"You asshole! You did have sex with that girl... didn't you?" Erica yelled out loud enough for other people to hear.

When she asked this question, I hung my head, feeling ashamed and distraught with no hope of alleviating her anger. I couldn't mindfully answer any of her questions, and it had become evident that she already knew the answers to most of them. There was no way I could have fabricated an explanation at this point that could reverse what had already happened.

Explaining the truth in a way that could have justified my actions would have taken the combined efforts of a philosopher, a psychiatrist, and a perfect gentleman. If some worldly miracle had occurred, and I had suddenly inherited each of these attributes, I still wouldn't have been able to gain back the lost purity in our relationship. I stood there without a response that was worth being said for a long enough time that Erica eventually decided to walk away. When I realized she had no intentions of returning to the void explanation in our one-sided conversation, I yelled, "Erica, come back... I'm sorry," but she never turned around.

This disheartening image I have of her walking away from me with such anger and strong convictions of distrust remained in the back of my head for years after that night. It suddenly felt as if all of the nails holding the framework of our relationship together had been yanked out and stuck into my heart. I stood there crying and feeling horrible about what I had done for several minutes. For some reason, Sherly stood beside me for the entire time. She witnessed everything that happened. At first, she attempted to leave with Erica, but I knew my girlfriend well enough to know that she wanted to be alone.

"I'm sorry, Oliver," Sherly said, "but that is just the way Erica is."

"Yeah, I know. Once I realized how upset she was about all this, it wasn't hard to understand why she walked away. I just wish I knew whether or not she was coming back," I said, wiping the tears from my eyes. "I honestly didn't mean for this to happen... I swear to God."

"What happened, anyway?" Sherly asked. "Did you really have sex with that guy's girlfriend?"

"I don't know, sort of," I replied. "I was really drunk after Adam's party, and we happened to be running away from the cops at the same time. One thing just led to another."

"So, what... your dick just tripped and fell into her pussy, and there was nothing you could do about it?"

"Pretty much," I answered. "We didn't plan to get intimate... it just happened. We were both feeling bad about our relationships when I began to walk her home that night. The next thing I knew, we were lying down in the middle of the park, making out. Besides that, I thought Erica and I were broken up at the time."

"Man, that is so lame... and not even close to a good excuse," Sherly responded. "You better come up with something better to tell Erica... because if you tell her what you just told me, she's gonna hate your guts forever."

"Do you think she will forgive me if I come up with something better to say?"

"I don't know," Sherly responded. "Your relationship hasn't exactly been going smooth lately, and Erica is really pissed off at you right now."

"Can you do me a favor and not tell her what I told you? I need to think about what I am going to say to her, I said in desperation. I at least want to be given a fair chance to work things out with her.

"Don't worry. I won't say a word to her about this conversation, but you better think hard about what you plan to say to her because if you just come up with a bullshit excuse and a lame-ass apology, she's not going to just break up with your sorry ass, she'll probably cut your dick off," Sherly said. "So anyway, do you need a ride home?"

"I suppose so," I answered. "It's not like I want to stay here, and my house is on the other side of town."

I woke up the following morning to a horrible feeling of anxiety, which only got worse as the morning went on. As I began to understand better what happened the night before, the anxiety in my chest turned into a full-blown panic attack, which made it difficult to stand up for any significant amount of time without getting dizzy. I just laid down on my bed and concentrated on taking deep breaths to regain comfort with reality.

Once the dizzy feeling finally went away, I attempted to call Erica. I didn't have anything planned to say to her, so I made this call more out of impulse than sound reason. I probably dodged a bullet when she didn't answer her phone, but that wasn't how I felt about it at the time. I ended up calling her three more times that morning before I finally gave up for the day.

Unfortunately, these failures to connect with Erica only made my day worse. I knew that I had made an irreversible mistake, whether Erica ever decided to forgive me or not. This heartbreaking realization was manifested through broken promises, guilty feelings, and a general lack of respect for my relationship. I told Erica many lies the night before, mostly white in color, but the ones that weren't so plain ironically revealed the honest truth about the epic sexual blunder I made.

The sanctity of our commitment to one another would be damaged forever, regardless of whether it was eventually repaired enough to move forward with our relationship. However, this wasn't what was on my mind that morning or for many days that followed because this disheartening epiphany could only be realized after a significant amount of forgiveness transpired. Unfortunately, before the healing process could begin, we would have to come to terms with my broken promises and a compromised commitment to an otherwise flawless relationship.

I may not have even come close to understanding any of this before I went to bed that night. What I did understand was that I could do nothing to expedite forgiveness or end the argument of betrayal without giving Erica some space. From time to time, these thoughts of hopeful forgiveness were interrupted by profound regret and a solid chance that Erica wouldn't ever trust me again or want to continue our relationship. These thoughts were terrifying and impossible to avoid.

I called Erica several times for a week or so without making a single connection. This made me feel worse and worse with each day that went by. I spent this time mostly in solitude, playing video games and writing love letters to Erica. The letters I sent her expressed my love and were very thorough about not wanting this fight to end our relationship. I also attempted to pacify the gray area infidelity caused by my romantic endeavor with the blond-haired girl in the park by explaining that we didn't actually have sex. Then, I wrote a poem and drew a picture for her, which I included with the last love letter I wrote before finally giving up on this line of communication as well.

I'm bound to my creative tower
Leaving reality, I lost my power
I want to feel and leave you breathless
Helpless and restless, I ponder from afar
Shall I wish upon this giant star
Which continues to shine so very bright
Or use its light to cast my shadow on your tower wall
To remember me always, once and for all

Deeper I fall as I continue to wait
Holding this heart-shaped question written by fate
Ironically belated the clever question clearly stated
This was not to be asked unless the heart was true
Because the answers you seek will not be given to you
Cautiously take this little clue placed in rhythm and rhyme
And the question will answer itself when it is time
There it will remain forever and always revealed
Not as much hidden as perfectly concealed

The answer itself will truly destine
The time it will take to enlighten this question
Then the present will reflect upon its past
As the future decides how long it will last
By evaluating the beauty within
While tempting is resistance to sin
Over and over again my day began waiting for the sun to rise
Merely a star, but much bigger in size
Upon this sunny day, I wished I may, I wish I might
A much bigger wish then the first star I would see that night
Quiet and poised I asked the giant light
To grant my wish I'd make again that night

In this tower of regret
I waited for the sun to set
From dawn till dusk, I pondered from afar
Finally, the night revealed the light of the brightest star
I wish I may, I wish I might
Upon the star that shined so bright
All I wish is that your wish come true this night

Chapter XIV

I ENDED MY WEEK of solitude by asking Billy to borrow his computer for a few days. My intentions were to learn more about the dark web and the evil person who exploited Erica. Unfortunately, I spent roughly twenty-four hours staring at the computer while searching the dark web without learning anything about black market crimes or my evil nemesis. However, I did find dozens of pictures and videos of Erica, along with several of the other kids he had victimized. Some of these kids were little boys and girls as early as ten years old, which was traumatizing to see or think about.

Finally, after spending three days searching for information about who was responsible for exploiting Erica and the other victims of similar cybercrimes, I stumbled upon a way to contact this evil person through an encrypted email address. The website that I found didn't reveal who this person was. It just provided contact information to download the videos and pictures of the exploited adolescents to private computers.

I could have written the sick fucker an email, but I stopped well short of doing so because I couldn't come up with a plan to initiate a conversation without drawing suspicion. I also figured a criminal of this caliber had a screening process that would not be easily penetrated without a good reason and an awful lot of luck.

Unfortunately, I ended up returning Billy's computer without any idea how Erica had ended up in her situation, but I was still incredibly determined to figure it out.

I thought of going to the police with the information I had about this evil person, but I decided against this for a couple of reasons. The first reason was that I hated law enforcement and didn't want them to be the ones who executed my revenge. My revenge was personal, so I decided that if I ever got law enforcement involved, it would only be after I removed his genitals or something of this nature.

The second reason was that I didn't know how turning this matter over to law enforcement would impact Erica. Our town was small, and there was little chance that rumors wouldn't somehow spread about Erica's exploitation if this were to occur. This meant that not only would she be dealing with the trauma of being a victim of cyber exploitation for the rest of her life, but she would also have to deal with the fact that everyone she knew would know about it. Erica was a delicate flower and had very thin skin, so I thought she would be better off never knowing how extensive her cyber exploitation was. This was the main reason that I didn't get the police involved in this matter.

As if the past week or so hadn't been shitty enough already, what happened the day I returned Billy's computer would make things substantially worse. The morning started with a phone call from the Ogallala police department. Apparently, several eyewitnesses saw Billy and I helping Adam drag the fat, dead guy out of Adam's apartment. The officer said that there were no charges that we were being faced with at that time, but he insisted that we could be held as an accomplice in the future if we didn't provide statements to help further incriminate our friend.

I felt that the officer's request was super shady, so I said that this matter would have to be discussed with my parents before I agreed to come to the police station. I wouldn't have had a problem telling him my side of the story, but he didn't seem interested in the truth or what I had to say about the situation if it didn't falsely describe Adam's criminal intent to murder the alleged victim in his case.

Once I got off the phone with the police officer, I called Billy to let him know I was going to his farm to return his computer. However, the moment his phone was answered, he immediately began to tell me about a similar call that he had received from the officer who had spoken to me. I could tell by the sound in his voice that he seemed substantially more worried about the situation than I was. From what he explained, the officer was significantly more threatening and demanding with Billy than he was with me.

After discussing what the police had said to one another, Billy asked me if I wanted to take a cruise and smoke a joint. I really didn't feel up to it and just wanted to return his computer so I'd be done with commitments for the day. Nevertheless, I could tell he was super stressed, so I decided to be a good friend and hang out with him for a little while. I told him that I was about to leave for his farm, but he insisted on picking me up in his father's old, redneck farm truck.

When Billy pulled up to my house twenty minutes later, I could hear the AM radio playing shit-kicking country music out of one little dash speaker, and it sounded terrible. I was surprised to see him driving this piece of shit because he had just bought a brand-new 2001 Dodge Ram pickup truck. When I asked where his new truck was, he said it was in the shop getting lifted, and some bigger tires were being put on it. I could smell booze on his breath when he said this, and it became apparent that he was pretty intoxicated as we headed out of town.

"So, what's up?" I asked.

"Dude, this shit is so fucked up!" Billy responded. "I have a really bad feeling about this."

"About what?"

"About being an accomplice to murder. What do you think?"

"Dude, this is all bullshit," I told him. "They're just trying to get under our skin."

"Well, it's working!" Billy replied.

"Just settle down, dude. I'm sure everything will be all right," I responded.

"I sure hope so!"

Billy turned down a gravel road after a short cruise down the highway. A few minutes later, he turned onto a jeep trail leading into a wheat field. It was only mid-summer, so the field was green instead of golden like it would be in the fall. We finally stopped in the middle of this field to smoke a joint, and then Billy grabbed a few things from a small cooler in the back of the truck. When he returned to the cab, he was holding a large tequila bottle in one hand and two zip-lock bags full of drugs in the other.

"Here, take a swig," Billy said, as he handed me the bottle of tequila.

"Okay, but I'm not looking to get shitfaced today."

"You do you, Oliver, but check this out!" Billy replied, holding up a large bag of weed in one hand and what appeared to be hallucinogenic mushrooms in the other.

"Holy shit, dude," I responded after taking a swig of tequila. "What the fuck... is that mushrooms?"

"Yep, you are looking at a fat-ass bag of cyclicibe cubensis hallucinogenic mushrooms."

"Where the fuck did you get that?" I asked.

"These came straight out of an aquarium in my basement," Billy replied. "I've been working on a new project inspired by High Times magazine and some genius out in Washington who put together a cookbook called PF. You have no idea how easy it is to grow these little fuckers"

"No shit! It looks like it."

"So... do you want to dose?"

"Dose?"

"Yeah, do you want to trip?" Billy asked.

"On mushrooms?"

"No, on LSD... duh... yeah, do you want to eat some mushrooms?"

"I guess so," I said, not fully understanding what was on his mind.

Billy reached into the bag and handed me five little mushrooms. I held them in my hand for a minute, observing what I was about to eat. These mushrooms looked vastly different from what I had seen sitting beside the orange pinto at the Phish concert. They were all dried, almost crispy, and looked gnarly as hell. They had orangish-yellow caps and a sort of peach-colored stem. The stems were also tinted with a blueish color with little specs of purple all over them. On the bottom of the mushrooms was this soft white stuff with a little bit of a shiny, brownish-colored substance sticking to it.

"What the hell is this?" I asked, pointing to the bottom of the stem.

"That white shit is mycelium, and the shiny brown shit is ver-miculite."

"What the hell is that?"

"These little bastards grow from white shit called mycelium, and vermiculite is one of the ingredients you use to grow fungus."

"Dude, are you sure these are safe to eat?" I asked, slightly concerned.

"Safe... fuck yeah, they're safe to eat... if you swallow what is in your hand, I can guarantee that you will safely trip your balls off," he said with a grin.

"What is it like?"

"More or less, you just laugh like hell because everything looks funny," Billy replied. "Just eat them, and you'll see how awesome they are."

"Okay," I said, putting all five mushrooms in my mouth. They tasted terrible! These mushrooms may have been the most disgusting thing I had ever eaten in my life! It felt like I was chewing rubber marshmallows flavored with dog shit or something, and I almost threw up when I tried to swallow them.

"Here, wash them down with a swig of tequila," Billy said, as he handed over the bottle of booze while giggling. "They're pretty gross, huh?"

"Fuck yeah, they are!" I replied. "I'm not going to wash them down with no goddamned tequila... I have a bottle of coke in your truck."

"Dude, we need to get our story straight about this murder bullshit," Billy said when he saw me return from the truck with a bottle of soda in my hand.

"Okay," I replied, "so what's our story gonna be?"

"All we need to say is that we were hanging out in the courtyard and didn't know what even happened. We came upstairs when we heard yelling, and by then, it was all over. Adam asked us to help get the fat ass out of his apartment. We saw that he was knocked out, but he was obviously still breathing. We have to explain that we didn't know he was dead. That is the actual truth. I didn't know he was dead... did you?"

"Sure, fine, whatever." I replied, trying not to puke from the nasty taste of hallucinogenic mushrooms.

"Seriously, dude, we need to have our story straight!"

"Okay, but that asshole officer that we talked to isn't interested in the truth. He wants us to lie our asses off to make sure Adam gets convicted of murder."

"Good point!" Billy replied, while chewing on another mushroom. "Well then, what the fuck do you think we should tell them?"

"I don't know. Give me a minute, and I will think of something," I said, as I suddenly heard the spoken word of Johnny Cash being amplified through the shitty stereo in Billy's crappy ass truck. I listened to Johnny Cash sing a million songs while growing up, but I never understood the full range of emotions that went into his songs. Billy and I listened to the whole Folsom Prison album that afternoon, and the spoken words of Johnny Cash really got to me. It suddenly felt like I knew who Johnny Cash was. Even though I had memorized every lyric he sang, I never experienced a connection to his spoken words and music like I did that day.

"Nobody could ever replace Luther Perkins. How about one big cheer for Luther Perkins... I was going to do a song called San Quentin. Hey, there is a little kit back there, where I got all my dope, I mean, where I got all my things. There is a little red notebook back there. Will one of the guards bring it to me? It's in that briefcase back there that has all the songs I stole in it.... I'm telling it like it is... ain't I? I wrote a song yester-day. I tried... It takes a lot of imagination sometimes to write a song and really put something into it that somebody will understand... we have been in several prisons... Folsom Prison, San Quentin, and Starkville, Mississippi jail. You wouldn't believe it... one time, I got thrown into jail for picking flowers. You can't hardly win, can you? God damn... No telling what they'd do if you picked an apple or something. Well, I would like to sing this song for you to get back at whoever you want to out there. In my case, I would like to get back at the fellow down in Starkville, Mississippi jail, that still has my thirty-six dollars." -Live at San Quentin, Johnny Cash 1969

Billy and I listened to the music of Johnny Cash and a faint whistling sound blowing through the wheat field for several minutes before Billy eventually interrupted this prolonged moment of peaceful serenity, "Do you want to smoke a bowl?"

"Okay," I replied. We never said a word as that bowl was smoked. We just stared at the stereo in Billy's shitty truck and continued to listen to Johnny Cash. Finally, I said, "Johnny Cash rules."

"Yeah, some of the things he says..." Billy replied.

"I love listening to him talk. He's just awesome to listen to."

"Dude, you're starting to trip, but if you really want to hear some fucked up shit, you should listen to the record, Holy Land. He talks about all this holy shit, but really, I think he is saying something else. It is like there is an underlying meaning to what he says."

"Really... like what?" I asked, as the knobs on the radio began to spin in a psychedelic circle next to the little green tuner light, which suddenly looked brighter and oddly illuminated.

"He is describing a man, referring to Jesus," Billy explained. "He talks about the three wise men, Mt. Olives, the gate of Yosemite. Then he talks about how Jesus knew his divine purpose, and the night before he died, he knew that his hour had come. Johnny says that Jesus was born human, and just like anyone, he didn't want to die. In fact, he asked to be spared, and when they came to arrest him, he said, "I am he, whom you seek." He also talks about Sha Drack, Me Shack, and A-Bed-Nego, who walked out from the fires of hell. There was a spirit protecting these men, and the form of the fourth was like the son of God."

"What is that supposed to mean," I asked.

"Dude, it's so deep," Billy said, while staring into space.

"Do you have that album with you?"

"Hell no, that shit is only on vinyl."

"Huh?" I replied, suddenly feeling strangely perplexed by the wheat field and the cracks in the windshield. I listened to the rhythm of the songs that Johnny Cash sang, and it all seemed to be in sync with the sway of the wind blowing the plants around. I felt this wind through the open window, almost as if it were blowing right through me. A moment later, the world seemed to turn sideways, so I turned my head to compensate for this. Then the world appeared to turn upside down, almost completing a circle, so I turned my head back the other way and closed my eyes.

When I opened my eyes, I saw an incredible psychedelic vision. Bright elastic images appeared from the void of oblivion and stretched across an expanded peripheral depth of field. Then, colorful images and strange rubber-like shapes emerged from the wheat field, and other images fell from the sky. The madness of this moment inspired me to get out of the truck and interact with my hallucinations.

I almost fell as I stepped out of the vehicle because the ground was further down than it usually was, but it seemed closer than it typically appeared. It was impossible for my legs to compensate for this paradox, so I just wobbled around through the wheat field until I found a place to lie down. I saw the fluffiest clouds I had ever seen in my life from this perspective. Then, it appeared that the sky was falling, which I found to be profoundly hilarious. This caused me to laugh... uncontrollably... for nearly an hour.

Suddenly, this hysterical experience turned into an agitated feeling of paranoia... I felt suspicious of everything... the dirt in the ground, the wheat in the field, the sun in the sky, the heart in my chest, the soul in my body, the brain in my head... I was losing my mind! After experiencing several minutes of distress and troubling paranoia, all at once, these disturbing thoughts suddenly stopped. At this point, I began to stumble my way back to the truck, and I found Billy still sitting in the driver's seat, staring at absolutely nothing as if it were the most fantastic thing he had ever seen. I interrupted his moment of peculiar zen by asking, "How long does this last?"

"I don't know," Billy replied. This is the first time I've ever eaten this many mushrooms. Take a shot of tequila. It will make you feel better."

"How many mushrooms do you usually take?" I asked.

"One."

"One... what do you mean, one?"

"These particular mushrooms are a powerful psychedelic drug, Oliver. All you need is one."

"What the fuck?" I yelled. "You gave me five. I ate five... not one!"

"I know... isn't it awesome?"

"What if we stay this way forever?"

Billy looked over at me and calmly said, "That would be so fucking cool." Looking into his eyes, I could tell he meant what he said. Whether this was a calculated thought or not, it didn't sound very comforting. Moments later, I suddenly felt sick in the strangest way imaginable, which caused me to puke uncontrollably all over the side of the truck for several minutes as everything that I had ever eaten in my life was being emptied from my stomach.

I approached Billy again for insight regarding our descent into psychedelic mushroom madness, but I found him in no condition to answer my questions. He was sitting in his truck doing nothing...

I mean absolutely nothing at all. He didn't move, he didn't say anything, he didn't even blink. So, I decided to sit beside him in the passenger seat till he snapped out of it. Over the next several minutes, I watched the sunset on the horizon. This was when I realized that I was facing west, which was the first sane thought I was able to think all afternoon. Following this realization, the framework of reality was rebuilt one thought at a time... until they were no longer crazy.

Once the sun set over the horizon, I looked over at Billy and saw that he had passed out. After eating handfuls of mushrooms, smoking bowl after bowl, and slamming over half the handle of tequila, my friend was now sleeping. I was ready to go home at this point, so I nudged him, saying, "Billy... wake up!"

"Huh, holy shit! I just had the most fucked up dream ever," Billy replied the moment he opened his eyes.

"Dude, let's get out of here."

"Yeah... let's go," he replied, grabbing the tequila bottle. As he started the engine, he began to slam what was left of the bottle, which was a considerable amount of alcohol to drink, especially since he had drunk most of the bottle already.

"Christ, man... take it easy. We still need to get home!" I said.

"Yo, you would not believe the dream I just had," he said, just before spinning a broody back onto the jeep trail. "Holy shit, that dream was fucked up!"

"What was so fucked up about it," I asked, deeply concerned about his ability to drive as he began to accelerate down a dimly lit, hazard-ridden road. I had been in the same vehicle as Billy many times while driving drunk and never had a problem with it, but it was painfully obvious that he was way more fucked up than usual.

"Dude... I dreamt I was a giant mushroom having a dream. I dreamt that I was dreaming in a dream...and it was crazy! I was in a forest with a bunch of other mushrooms and was picked up by Big Bird from Sesame Street. Then, he gave me to the Count, who started counting mushrooms. One mushroom... ah...ha... ha... aaa, two, two mushrooms... ha... ah... ha...aaa, three, three mushrooms... ha... ha...ah...aaa, but the thing was... there weren't three mushrooms. There was only me... that's how fucked up this dream was."

"Dude, watch it...that turn is coming up here soon!" I said while putting on my seat belt.

"I know, I know, I see it," Billy said, badly slurring his speech. "Any who... where was I? Oh yeah, so then all of a sudden, the Count from Sesame Street turned into Homer from the Simpson's and said, 'mmm... mushrooms."

"Jesus Christ, dude... slow down! There is the turn!" I said, seeing the turn getting closer, but Billy showed no signs of slowing down.

"Yeah, yeah, yeah, I see it... stop interrupting me," Billy said, turning so hard that he almost rolled the truck into the ditch.

"Dude, let me drive," I demanded. "You're going to fucking kill us!"

"No, I'm not... just let me drive and listen to me... okay," he said, as he continued to accelerate. "Anywho... Homer ate me, and I saw life through Homer's eyes... and man... it was so awesome! I was yellow and only had three fingers... and one thumb... and the first thing I thought about was going home and fucking Marge, but when I got there... hey, where is the pipe?" Billy said, looking down at the bucket seat between us. "Let's smoke a bowl."

"Just let me look for it because you need to concentrate on driving," I replied.

"What the hell was I just talking about?" Billy asked.

"Fucking Marge or something about Sesame Street... I don't know?"

"That's right," Billy said, as he suddenly jerked the steering wheel and slammed on the brakes. "Fuuuuuck...meeeee..."

I looked up just before the truck hit the approach onto the pavement of the highway, and all I saw were headlights heading toward us at an incredible speed. Billy's desperate attempt to avoid collision sent the truck flying sideways onto the highway and into the broadside of a minivan! I heard tires squealing, car horns honking, and terrifying screams coming from all directions as the truck spun around and flew into the ditch.

When the vehicle finally stopped, I realized that I was incredibly fortunate to be wearing my seatbelt, which miraculously kept me in the passenger seat of the pickup truck without injury. Unfortunately, this feeling of peculiar fortune quickly dissolved into a catastrophe when I looked over and saw Billy's lifeless body and bloody face smashed into the metal steering wheel. I impulsively began to scream when I pulled his head back from the steering wheel and saw blood pouring out from his head. This was such a terrible sight to see that I went into a state of shock moments later, and I had no recollection of the next several minutes.

My blacked-out mind suddenly snapped back into reality when I heard sirens from approaching emergency vehicles. Entirely out of impulse, I grabbed the zip-lock bags full of mushrooms and weed, intending to hide the drugs before the cops showed up. In a state of panic, I ran into the dark field when I saw the lights from emergency vehicles getting close.

Unfortunately, two police cars quickly arrived at the scene, and I was immediately caught in the middle of the field by spotlights before I even had a chance to ditch the drugs. I tried to inconspicuously drop the two zip-lock bags before I put my hands in the air, but they fell only a couple of feet away from where I stood, so the police officers quickly found the drugs when they walked out into the field to question me. Surprisingly, they didn't say much about this and just threw me in the back of their cruiser until the paramedics could examine me.

I watched from the back seat of the police cruiser as more paramedics, police officers, and firefighters arrived at the scene. From what I could see, this accident was much worse than I had initially thought. The truck hit the minivan so hard that the van flew across the road and was utterly demolished. It was now flipped upside down in the ditch a hundred feet away. Unfortunately, it appeared that rural Nebraska didn't have enough ambulances or paramedics to efficiently respond to this horrific accident because it took four hours to get everyone into ambulances.

I was the very last person they examined. I could feel an abrasion on my face, minor whiplash, and pain across my chest from the seat belt, but it didn't feel like I had any severe injuries. I told the paramedics I felt okay and probably didn't need medical attention. Nevertheless, I was still put into an ambulance and transported to the hospital in Ogallala. I frantically asked if Billy would be all right as I was transferred from the back of the police car to the emergency vehicle, but I didn't get any answers. Since I was the last person transported, I witnessed the entire emergency response effort from the back seat of that police car that night, and what I saw would undoubtedly traumatize me for life.

Chapter XV

ONCE I ARRIVED AT the hospital, my injuries were looked at more closely. I got bandaged up and was given a neck brace for my whiplash, but I didn't suffer any life-threatening injuries. My parents came to the hospital that night as soon as they heard what had happened. They started asking me questions I didn't want to answer, so I pretended to be more out of it than I actually was. Incidentally, this may have been one of the main factors that contributed to the doctor's decision to have me spend the night.

It was pretty late to make phone calls, but I asked my parents to contact Erica to tell her about what had happened. Just after midnight, she came down after receiving this call. I could tell she was genuinely concerned about me, which made me feel better. However, her stay was short because we both were incredibly worried about Billy, so I encouraged her to investigate Billy's condition.

Unfortunately, we never found out how our friend was doing that night. Erica eventually returned to tell me that she had asked all the nurses and the front desk administration personnel if anyone named Billy had been treated in the hospital, and she was told that there was no one by that name being treated. I fell asleep a short while later, feeling utterly exhausted, but I still struggled to get a good night's sleep because I was constantly waking up from horrible nightmares, and each time, it seemed a little harder to get back to sleep.

The following morning, I found myself trapped in a real-life nightmare when a nurse and two police officers woke me up. I had no idea what to expect from this peculiar company, but I instantly got a bad feeling in my stomach about the situation. One of the officers sat on a chair beside the bed and forced me to engage in a very uncomfortable conversation. "Listen, Oliver, I hate to ruin your day, but I have some bad news," the officer said.

"Please don't tell me that my best friend is dead," I replied.

"No, fortunately, your friend survived the accident. However, he is in critical condition and is in a trauma center in Denver. He lost a lot of blood, broke his nose, and suffered a severe traumatic brain injury."

"Oh my God!" I responded, relieved that Billy wasn't dead but anxiously concerned about how badly he was hurt.

"About the minivan that you and your friend ran into... it contained a family of five traveling through town from Michigan. They were coming here to visit some relatives that live in Ogallala, and well... they never made it to their destination," the officer said with a somber tone.

"What happened to them?" I asked.

"Unfortunately, they were all hurt! Two of the children were little girls who were sitting in child safety seats, and it sounded like they would pull through with no life-threatening injuries. However, their younger brother and father are in critical condition and had to be flown out to two different hospitals. The boy went to the same Critical Care Trauma Center in Denver as your friend. The father was flown to Omaha to treat several critical injuries as well, but he is at least conscious... but the mother, who was in the passenger seat... she was ejected through the front window of the vehicle and died instantly. They found her body fifty feet from the van lying in the road with a crushed skull which was partially severed from her body just below the chin."

I didn't know what to say. I just stared blankly at this man, deeply troubled by what I had just heard. After sitting through a very eerie moment of silence, I began to feel a sharp pain shooting through my chest, "So what is going to happen?"

"Well," the officer said, taking a deep breath. "The reason why we are here is that we found two bags of drugs where we found you standing in the field last night. Do you know anything about this?"

"No, I don't," I said, shaking my head.

"I don't know if you're suffering from memory loss or what, but I was one of the officers who personally saw you drop these bags in the field while shining my spotlight on you. So, you are saying that you know nothing about this?"

"No, I really don't. I don't remember too much of anything from last night," I said, trying to buy some time to fabricate better lies that would get me out of this situation.

"I wish I didn't have to tell you this, but we have to take you to jail as soon as you are released from the hospital."

"For what?" I asked, feeling very nervous about the officer's comment.

"Possession of a controlled substance, and potentially for an accomplice to murder. I would consider yourself lucky because it turns out that your buddy Billy is facing many more charges than you."

"Like what?" I asked. "We weren't doing anything but driving down the road. That minivan came flying out of nowhere. It is not like he was trying to hit that vehicle."

"Well, let's see here," he said, as he took a small notebook out of his pocket. "It looks like he broke one, two, three.... about twelve laws he... maybe thirteen. The police chief hasn't decided yet if we plan to charge him with second-degree murder. That would be one hell of a coincidence if your two best friends were both accused of murder, and you were at the scene of both crimes but had nothing to do with either one of them.

It looks like you and your buddies have found yourself in the middle of a criminal triangle, considering that your friend Adam is still not cooperating with us and is refusing to accept a plea bargain of first-degree assault and manslaughter rather than face the consequences of being found guilty of second-degree murder. He seems to want to bring these matters to trial. Since he is not willing to accept full responsibility for this murder, the police chief has decided that both you and your buddy Billy should be charged as an accomplice to second-degree murder. That means along with the crimes you are facing from last night, you could be facing twenty years or more in prison."

"That's bullshit!" I yelled. "Those bags of drugs were not mine. I had absolutely nothing to do with the death of anyone!"

"According to several eyewitnesses, you helped carry that obese man out of Adam's apartment," the officer explained. "Unfortunately, this means that we have to put you under arrest for being an accomplice to that crime. You're also being charged as an accomplice to some of the crimes committed by your buddy, Billy. This would be in addition to your drug possession... unless you want to tell me about some things."

"Like what?" I asked.

"For starters, tell me about the drugs you dropped in the field?" the officer asked. "Where did you get them from?"

"I didn't drop any drugs in a field," I replied. "You had to be seeing things!"

"I saw with my own eyes that you were holding the bags before they were found," the officer explained. "I personally walked out into that field last night and wasn't surprised to find them lying on the ground exactly where I saw you drop them."

"I am going straight to jail after I'm released from the hospital?" I asked, feeling incredibly disturbed by what he had just told me.

"Looks that way," the officer replied.

"When am I going to get out of here?" I asked, frantically looking at the nurse.

"Your doctor has given me permission to release you right now," the nurse responded.

Immediately after she said this, the officer read me my rights. Then, the other officer helped me out of my bed and reached for my hands, but I pulled away and ducked into the corner of the hospital room. When I did this, he responded with a firm voice, "We can do this the easy way or the hard way... it is up to you. Either way, you are going to the city jail with us, at least until this mess you have gotten yourself into gets cleaned up."

At that point, I realized there was nothing I could say or do to change the inevitable outcome of going to the city jail that day. I didn't make any further attempt to resist my arrest after this. I was then placed in handcuffs for the first time in my life. This experience left me scared as hell as I was escorted down the hallway and out the front doors of the hospital.

I didn't say anything through this process until I walked toward the cop car. This was when I saw my parents pull into the parking lot, so I asked the officers if they could wait a minute for me to explain to my parents why I was being placed under arrest. Although they carried the persona of being two redneck assholes with no conscience, they did allow me to have a very brief conversation with my parents before bringing me to the police station.

I told them what was happening and downplayed the reason for my arrest. Unfortunately, the cops filled in a few more details, but this conversation was short and still left out a lot of content about the situation. At this point, my parents were more confused than I was about my arrest. Before I was placed into the cop car, my parents asked, "So what will it cost to bail him out?"

"That has not been determined yet," the officer responded. "It depends on how cooperative your son is. If he cooperates and answers our questions, then it may not be much at all."

"What do you mean?" my dad asked.

"Oliver and I will discuss a few things when we get to the police department," the officer explained. "I will let you know what happens."

Following this statement, I was put in the back seat of the cop car and taken into police custody. When we arrived at the station, I was led into a little room with nothing but a table and a few chairs in it. Once the officers finished escorting me into this room and the door was closed, an officer started to take off my handcuffs. This is when I asked, "How long will I be in here?"

"That depends on you," the officer replied before he proceeded to ask me several questions concerning my arrest. However, I quickly decided to exercise my right to remain silent out of fear that my responses could further incriminate myself and my friends. Then, the police officer started a one-sided conversation with me by saying he already knew the answers to everything he would ask me. I knew right then and there that everything that would come out of his mouth following this comment was going to be total bullshit, but this didn't mean I wasn't afraid of what he was going to say.

He began by asking me what Billy and I were doing before the accident. He tried to get me to describe the events that had led up to this, but I didn't answer any of these questions. I just sat there with my arms crossed. I had nothing to say to him and could tell that this was really pissing him off. At this point, he decided to change the subject by asking me about the drugs that he had found.

"Look, Oliver, I know you are a good kid and come from a good family, but you are facing serious charges here. I know that you don't want to be locked up in a jail cell for twenty years, and that is what this may come down to unless you start giving me some answers. Now, you can tell me about these crimes and be let out in a few days, or else you'll have to suffer some serious consequences."

I continued to remain silent and just stared at him with a blank expression on my face. I didn't want to answer his questions... I didn't know how to answer his questions even if I wanted to. Plus, I was enjoying the fact that I was pissing this guy off. The more this man would talk, the more I began to despise him for the position he was trying to put me in, and the more I didn't talk, the more upset he became. After asking me over and over about the accident, the drugs, and what had happened at Adam's party, he really started to lose his shit.

The fact that he wanted me to answer his questions so badly had caused him to shove his foot in his mouth a little too far. This pig wanted me to rat on my friends, and I knew he was looking for a scapegoat. A fever pitch was finally reached after an hour of failed interrogation. I had upset him so much that he stood up with his face glowing red and yelled, "Just answer my questions, you little shit!"

Equally as angry, I acted impulsively as I stood up, yelling back, "It will be a cold day in hell before I answer your questions! There is something called friendship, built upon respect, honor, and trust, something you know nothing about! So, if you think I am going to sell out my friends, you can go fuck yourself!"

Saying this, I knew I was in for it! The officer suddenly threw me down on the floor and started to repeatedly kick me hard in my ass. Then, he dragged me by my foot through the doorway of the room and down the hallway. At the end of the hall was a large steel door, where we briefly stopped while he punched in a code to unlock it. After he kicked the door open, I was dragged down a flight of stairs. When we reached the bottom of the stairwell, I was dragged down a long hallway with several jail cells.

Oddly enough, the officer dragged me right past Adam's jail cell. Adam heard me yelling, "Fuck you asshole... let go of my foot!"

"Oliver, what the hell are you doing in here?" I looked over when Adam said this and saw him holding onto the steel bars of his cell, but I wasn't in a position to answer his question. Finally, the police officer let go of my foot and let me stand up when we reached the last jail cell at the end of the hallway. Once again, I heard Adam yell, "Oliver, what are you doing in here?"

"I don't know," I answered. "Ask this asshole cop!"

"Shut the fuck up... you little shit," The officer said, as he grabbed for his keys. "I hope you enjoyed the past eighteen years of your life because this will be your home for a long time."

"Fuck you!" I replied. "I'll be out by the end of the week, and you know it!"

As I said this, the officer opened the door to a jail barely big enough to fit a cot in it and shoved me onto its concrete floor. Then he locked the door behind him, leaving me trapped behind steel bars as he said, "You just made a big mistake, and you will pay for it! Now you have all the time in the world to think about what you said to me... and what you didn't say to me, for that matter!"

For five straight days, I never left the four walls of that cell. All the other inmates were let out for meals and exercise, but I was an exception. The only time I saw anybody was when an officer brought me my meals, which were so nasty that I didn't eat for three days, fearing that somebody had either spit on my food or pissed on my plate.

Most of the cells in this jailhouse were filled with drunk drivers or people who were only there for a few hours before they got bailed out. The rest of the inmates had cell mates they could talk to, but I was alone in the last cell of an exceedingly long hallway. Since there wasn't an inmate next to me, I couldn't talk with anyone without being heard by every inmate in the hallway. I only spoke to Adam when he or I would yell down the hallway, mainly to see if we were both still locked up.

This was my life while incarcerated in the Ogallala City Jail. I had nothing to do but stand up, sit down, and stare at the walls. The rest of the time, I was lying on my rock-hard bed, sleeping or staring at the ceiling. My dreams were the only entertainment I had. My imagination didn't seem to exist during my incarceration, which left me to experience nothing but utter boredom. The worst part about all of this was that I didn't have a clue how long I was going to be locked up.

During this time, I couldn't help but continuously reflect on the crimes that my friends and I were being accused of and how they affected me. These thoughts kept leading me back to the same bullshit realization, which was that I was being held in jail without being formally charged with anything. I felt like this was caused by a lack of probable cause and profound corruption of legal authority.

After repeatedly hashing through these thoughts, I came to other disturbing conclusions as well. The officer's vain attempt to hear my side of the story caused him to show some interesting emotions. I understood that he needed to gather facts and statements, particularly from me, because I was the prime witness to the crimes that Billy and Adam had committed.

I figured that if these matters were taken to trial, he probably wouldn't have enough solid evidence against my friends to win a court case without me. All he really knew was that these crimes had all happened, and I was somehow involved. However, he didn't have much evidence to prove how my involvement related to the crimes that Adam and Billy were accused of. If either Billy or Adam were eventually determined to be innocent, it would be a disaster for the

Ogallala police department because their charges created some of the most significant news stories in Ogallala's recent history.

To make matters worse, the accident that Billy and I were involved in nearly killed an entire family, which meant there was no possibility of sympathy when it came to blaming someone for this disaster. Also, everyone absolutely loved the fat kid that Adam punched at his party. He was arguably the most famous person who had ever lived in our town, besides a football player who went on to play for the Green Bay Packers in the seventies. Every time he participated in a contest, our local news televised it. This person wasn't just an unusually obese person. He was a local legend.

This undoubtedly put the chief of police in a precarious situation of losing his job if my friends were acquitted of the crimes that they were being accused of. He had to have conclusive evidence to ensure a guilty plea, and I was the ticket to solving this problem. I didn't have any idea how long I was going to be locked up, but I thought about these things obsessively the entire time.

Chapter XVI

In the afternoon of the fifth day behind bars, the same officer who had initially tossed me into my cell came to visit me. He said, "This could be your lucky day. I reached out to your parents, and they have the money for your bail, but only if the police chief decides to let you out on bond. I may be willing to help you out if you decide to cooperate with me."

"Okay," I said, excited that something was happening. At this point, I would have been content with someone handing me a ball or even a barbell, anything to distract me from the boredom and misery of being incarcerated. After the officer unlocked the door to my cell, I was put in handcuffs and led back down the hallway, again passing by Adam. I was then led up the stairs and back into the same room where I was brought to when I first came to the jailhouse.

When I walked into the room, I saw my parents sitting at the table. When they saw me, they immediately got up to give me a hug. After this emotional greeting, the officer sat me down in a chair in the corner of the room. "Your parents have decided to place an awful lot of trust in you by offering to put up money for your bail. This means you must return for your court date to prevent your parents from losing this money. With this said, these court dates have not been set just yet, and the reason for this is that your charges are pending on your willingness to cooperate with local law enforcement."

"Cooperate how?" I asked.

"We need you to provide some solid statements about the crimes you were involved in."

"What kind of statements?"

"What I mean is that you need to discuss some issues concerning the drugs that were found in the field the night of the accident and the events leading up to the crimes that you and your friends committed," the officer answered.

"What are my friends and I being charged with?"

The officer removed the same little notebook from his pocket that he referred to while I was in the hospital. After putting on some reading glasses, he said, "Your buddy, Billy, is facing four counts of vehicular assault, four counts of attempted manslaughter, four counts of reckless endangerment, one count of manslaughter, DUI, possession of a controlled substance, careless driving, not obeying a stop sign, driving with expired tags, driving with a suspended driver's license, and possession of a dangerous weapon while intoxicated. We are still waiting for him to get out of the hospital so we can interrogate him, but he will likely be facing second-degree murder, which is also what your friend Adam is charged with. This could result in them spending a lifetime in a Nebraska State Prison."

"What exactly am I being charged with?" I asked.

"That depends on the statements you provide," the officer answered.

"What happens if I don't provide the statements you want?"

"Well, you... you... umm... you will be charged with drug possession and potentially an accomplice to the murders your friends committed." The officer was not prepared to be asked this question and expressed a look of uncertainty as he stumbled over his words.

"Is my son being accused of felonies or misdemeanors?" my dad asked.

"They are likely felonies," the officer answered.

"Likely?" my dad responded.

"This all depends on how cooperative your son is. He may not be charged with anything if he gives me the answers I want to hear. I may be willing to offer your son a full pardon," the officer said, as he turned toward me. "This means that you will be completely free, and your parents won't even have to put up any bail. All you need to do is tell me where the drugs you had in your possession came from."

"Is that it?" I asked.

"No," the officer replied, "you will also need to answer some questions about the murders your friends committed."

"Let me guess...you plan to ask me questions about these crimes and expect answers that will incriminate my friends."

"Something like that," the officer replied.

"This doesn't sound like a very good deal to me. I don't have many friends, and you are asking me to incriminate my two best friends. How much time am I facing if I don't answer your questions?" I asked, thinking that the police department was being incredibly corrupt for putting me in this situation.

"You could be facing ten years in prison," the officer responded. "I also wouldn't recommend bringing these matters to trial because I am positive you will be found guilty."

"What makes you so sure?" I asked. "I thought that I was innocent until proven guilty."

With a grin, the officer responded, "Indeed you are, but in this case, you're guilty of crimes with special circumstances."

"Why is that?" I asked.

"Because I happened to be the arresting officer and a witness to some of the crimes you committed."

"So, you are going to prevent me from getting a fair trial?"

"I'm certainly going to try," the officer said with an evil grin.

"THE HELL YOU ARE!" my dad yelled as he stood up and leaned over the table between himself and the officer. My father's colossal frame, red face, and spit coming out of his mouth suddenly showed a level of rage few have ever encountered. Towering over the officer with uninhibited anger, my dad continued to yell, "MY BOY WILL GET A FAIR TRIAL WHETHER THE HELL YOU LIKE IT OR NOT! I don't know who the fuck you think you are, but you will NOT be standing in the way of justice... NOT in the state of Nebraska... NOT in the city of Ogallala... NOT in county court, and DEFINITELY NOT IN ANY ROOM WITH ME STANDING IN IT... AM I MAKING MYSELF CLEAR?"

"I understand," the officer said, severely intimidated by the fantastic fury my dad had just bestowed upon him.

"You better understand because I'm tired of listening to your bullshit! What you are asking my son to do is wrong! I don't care what you think the laws are around here, but I will not be putting up any bail money unless my son has been charged with a crime." As he said this, my dad grabbed the table with one hand and tossed it against the wall so hard that it busted into pieces that went flying all over the room. There were now only a few inches of separation between him and the officer, "NOW, GET THESE FUCKING HANDCUFFS OFF MY SON BEFORE I REALLY START TO GET MAD!"

"Holy shit! Settle down," the officer said, while holding up his hands as if to prevent my dad from hitting him.

"I will not settle down unless you release my son from custody and agree to give him some time to think about this bullshit offer of yours," my dad said, looking like he was ready to rip the officer's face off.

"Okay, holy shit," the officer responded as he continued to hold his hands up in front of this face. "Just give me a minute to have our secretary draw up an agreement."

"Well, get moving. My wife and I haven't eaten breakfast yet, and I tend to get a little irritable when I'm hungry," my dad said as he stepped back and opened the door for the officer.

"It's true... he gets a little irritable when he doesn't eat," my sweet mother said, speaking up for the first time. The officer looked at my mom like a deer in headlights when she said this and appeared to be crying as he removed the handcuffs from my wrists. He never made eye contact with me or my dad as he was walking out the door.

After the officer left, my parents and I sat in awkward silence for a couple of minutes before my mom said to me, "It breaks my heart to see you in this situation, but you'll be set free and won't have any crime on your record if you agree to cooperate with the officer... and your father and I will pay for you to go to any college you want in the state." Then she turned toward my dad, looking for confirmation, and said, "Right, Jim?" My dad unsurprisingly didn't answer, and after realizing he wasn't going to, my mom continued, "You won't have to live here anymore. You can make new friends, start a new future, and live a happy life away from all this."

I was apprehensive and hesitant to settle these matters with such malevolence and dishonesty. My dad O-B-V-I-O-U-S-L-Y understood this, but for some reason, a clear picture had not yet been painted for my mom. With a cross brow, I looked up at my mom and asked, "What happens if I don't agree to incriminate my friends... huh... Mom? What happens then?"

"I don't know what happens then," my mom answered, tossing her hands in the air and shaking her head. "I guess you will just sit in jail with your criminal buddies."

"Yeah, maybe so," I replied. The officer never returned to the room with the document I needed to sign. I'm positive this was because he was afraid of my father. He actually had the tenacity to send the jailhouse secretary into the room with an agreement to sign. The agreement gave me six days to decide if incriminating my friends was worth my freedom. I hated law enforcement for putting me in this situation. Nevertheless, I needed time to think about my decision, so I reluctantly signed it before we left.

July 7th, 2001

Deputy James O'Hare
Ogallala City Police Department
145 Main Street
Ogallala, Nebraska 65097

I, _____________________, consent to the following terms pending my release from custody from the Ogallala City Police Department. This agreement is an injunction with crimes committed within the jurisdiction of the Ogallala City Law Enforcement. I understand I must return to police custody by noon on July 13th. Any actions causing a breach of this agreement will be considered contempt of court, which will carry an additional mandatory sentence of six months of jail time under the strict supervision of Deputy James O'Hare.

Date: _____________________

Signature: _____________________

Chapter XVII

AFTER LEAVING OGALLALA CITY Jail, we drove home to pick up my sisters and went to the diner for breakfast. This may have been the strangest meal that my family ever ate together. Everyone knew how upset my dad was, which kept our conversation to a bare minimum. However, just before we left, my dad broke his silence for the first time since ripping the officer a new asshole when he said to me, "I would completely understand whatever decision you make about this, Oliver."

"We would?" my mom intently replied. "I thought we wanted Oliver to go to college."

"What your mother is trying to say is that if you don't agree to the officer's proposition, we will pay for a good defense attorney," my dad responded. "Either way, we would like you to go to college."

"Thanks, Dad," I replied, which ended our conversation.

I paced throughout the house for a while after returning home and then finally went down to my bedroom with my chest filled with anxiety. A heavy numbness left me feeling empty for several hours. This time offered deliverance from some of my feelings while locked in my cell, but it also brought new feelings into focus. The decisions that I was faced with soon created a psychological prison that felt worse than the lack of freedom of being in police custody.

Unsurprisingly, this situation made me want to see Erica more than anything else. I needed her to be here for me. Before deciding anything, I needed her advice, companionship, and her honest perspective about the situation. Unfortunately, I could not get in touch with her. After making a couple of phone calls, I drove by her house and the supermarket where she worked, hoping to see her car parked out in front, but I couldn't find her anywhere.

After two days of this, I eventually went to Sherly's house to see if she knew where to find Erica. When I pulled into Sherly's driveway, I saw her hanging clothes over a clothesline beside her house. As I exited my vehicle, she walked over to me and said, "Oliver, what are you doing here? I thought you were in jail!"

"I was in jail, but I got let out a couple of days ago," I responded.

"That's good. I thought that you might be in there for a while. Everybody in town has been talking about this accident, but nobody really knows what happened except what we heard on the news... so what happened... are you all right?"

"I'm fine," I replied, "but Billy is really fucked up!"

"That's what I heard on the news," Sherly said with an expression of inquiry, "What happened?"

"It's a long story, and I'm not supposed to talk about it with anyone until a few things get resolved. I will explain it all to you later. Anyway, do you know where Erica is?"

"She went to go visit her uncle in Grand Island to see if he had any money to put toward her father's heart transplant."

"That's just great! I really need to see her. Do you know when she'll be coming back?

"No, not exactly... she just said she'd be gone for a few days."

"How long ago was that?" I asked.

"She left yesterday morning."

"Shit! Well, at least that means she will be back in time."

"In time for what... why do you need to see her so bad?"

"I just need to... that's all."

"Well, can you tell me anything, or do I need to keep guessing about what's going on here?"

"Promise not to tell anyone?"

"I promise."

"Pinky promise," I said, holding out my pinky finger.

"Pinky promise," Sherly answered, as we linked fingers.

"Things are pretty fucked up right now."

"Yeah, I know."

"No, I mean really fucked up!" I replied. "My two best friends are being accused of murder, and I have to decide if I plan to cooperate with law enforcement. If I don't, then they say that I will be charged with drug possession and an accomplice to murder."

"Then cooperate with them," Sherly said. "Problem solved."

"It's not that easy," I replied. "They want me to say things to help convict Adam and Billy."

"Are you kidding me?"

"I wouldn't make this kind of shit up."

"What are you going to do?"

"I don't know?" I replied. "I just wish that I could talk with Erica about it first."

"I can't help you there," Sherly said. "She's still pretty upset with you. She's obviously concerned about you and the accident you were in, but I still don't know if she is ready to talk to you about anything yet."

"She did come to see me in the hospital, so maybe she has forgiven me," I said with a hopeful tone.

"Oliver, you fucked the high school quarterback's girlfriend," Sherly replied. "Trust me, she hasn't forgiven you."

"I didn't fuck her... we just fooled around is all," I said.

"Well, whatever... you may as well have fucked her. Either way, Erica is likely still too pissed off about it to want to talk to you."

"Yeah, you're probably right," I mumbled as I turned around, facing my car.

"Wait, Oliver, I want to know more about the accident," Sherly said.

"I don't really want to talk about that right now. I have to go. Maybe I'll tell you about it later."

"Okay," Sherly replied, "I'll let you know if I hear anything from Erica."

"Thanks, I'd appreciate that."

I drove off with an elevated feeling of frustration without a destination in mind. After driving aimlessly around town for a few minutes, I realized I had nowhere to go. Erica was out of town and hated my guts, while my two best friends were held hostage by our corrupt legal system, so I just decided to go home. My mother stood in the kitchen when I got there and asked if I wanted to eat lunch, but I told her I wasn't hungry. I just wanted to go down to my room and avoid having any conversation with my family that day.

After lying on my bed for several minutes, feeling confused and empty inside, I decided to write a letter to Erica to explain my situation. However, after writing for several hours, I never came up with anything that I felt comfortable giving to her. I just wanted to talk to Erica in person and hoped to get the opportunity to do so before returning to jail.

With only four more days to decide my fate, I had to define what friendship, freedom, and integrity meant to me. A bone-chilling terror presented itself within the option of freedom being offered to me. To avoid committing a crime of legality, I would need to commit a crime of integrity. This would not only be a crime of personal integrity but one that encompassed the integrity of my friendships.

After thoroughly thinking about the police department's proposal, I felt I had understood its purpose and what would happen if I agreed to the proposed conditions. If I wasn't put in jail by a guilty verdict in a court of law, my conscience would incarcerate me with a feeling of guilt that wouldn't be any better. The thought of carrying this guilt around with me for the rest of my life led me to a conclusive decision not to agree to what was being offered by local law enforcement.

I would empathize with my friends before sympathizing with my selfishness, but this wasn't the only decision I had to make. Considering the corruption in our legal system, I felt that it may be impossible for any of us to be found innocent. I had a strong prediction that this corruption would determine an ill fate for my friends and me no matter what I decided.

After hours of frustrating thoughts, I realized I didn't want to resolve this bizarre predicament by engaging in legal matters. This is when I came up with the answer to one of the most challenging decisions of my life. Whether it was the right decision or not, only time would tell, but I decided that I would flee from law enforcement and leave town. I didn't know where I planned to go or what this would mean for my future... I guess I just planned to figure my life out later.

Unfortunately, this decision would create several more problems. It was as if I was stuck in an enigma of terrible consequences no matter how I turned. This made me think that before I left, I would at least need to explain my actions to those directly involved with these crimes and to the people I loved the most as best I could. So, I decided to write four letters. One would be written to my parents, one to Adam, another to Billy, and one to Erica.

I spent all night writing these letters. This was incredibly emotional, but they were all finished by morning. My plan was now to go around town delivering the letters and to leave at some point that afternoon. So, shortly after sunrise, I went upstairs to get four envelopes and found my mother sitting at the kitchen table drinking coffee while putting a puzzle together. I wasn't expecting to see her up so early, but I guess I was never awake early enough to know when she usually woke up. She looked over at me when I looked through the kitchen drawers for an envelope.

"Good morning, Oliver. You are up early," my mom said.

"Yeah, I'm going to go fishing, I think, and the best time to catch walleye is early in the morning," I said, hoping my lie would pacify her suspicious nature.

"Oh, that sounds nice," she said just as I found the envelopes. I tried to sneak back downstairs before my mom asked me anything else about my plans for the day, but my goal was not attained because she asked, "So, have you decided what you plan to do about your legal situation with your friends?"

"Yeah, I think so, but I'm not entirely sure just yet. I'll let you know when I have it figured out, I said before running back down the stairs. When I returned to my room, I began to pack some of my things into a backpack so I'd be prepared to leave once the envelopes were delivered. It didn't take long to pack because the only things I managed to fit in my backpack were a few changes of clothes, my Leatherman tool, and a few notebooks. Then, I ran up the stairs as quietly as possible and exited through the garage door before my mother could say anything to me.

When I got in my car to deliver the letters, I instinctively drove out of town, going south toward Billy's house. However, as I started to drive down this road, it suddenly occurred to me that there wasn't any place where I could leave a letter for Billy. This caused me to think through a series of disturbing thoughts. I realized in this expressive moment that I may never see my best friend again. If he ever gained his consciousness back, he would be sent to prison no matter what, and from the charges that were described to me, he could spend the rest of his life behind bars. These thoughts and all that they encompassed suddenly hit me pretty hard. There had been so much going on that I didn't realize how much I loved this person and how much I would miss him not being in my life.

This was when a greedy thought occurred to me, or maybe it wasn't a greedy thought at all, but it was about something that I had to reconcile before I left Nebraska. I knew that Billy was worth at least two hundred thousand dollars before adding how much his ranch was worth. On top of an extensive list of assets, he had a giant marijuana field that eventually needed to be harvested. With good fortune and a lot of luck, the police wouldn't find this field before something more noble happened to it.

This made me think that Billy would not have access to anything he owned potentially for the rest of his life, including the cash he had stashed in his house. I thought about some of the conversations that I had with Billy, and I remember him describing a tunnel where he kept some of his valuables. When I was nine, I remember my father digging a passageway between our food storage and the storm cellar beside the house.

Billy told me he buried the storm cellar a few years back and turned it into a bunker for his valuables. I anticipated that this is where he likely kept his cash. About the time this thought was rendered, I turned onto the dirt road leading toward Billy's house without thinking about my next move. After an intense internal debate, I decided to look for the cash that was likely stashed at Billy's house. At this point, I still had no plans for what to do with this money if I found it... I think that I was curious more than anything.

When I arrived at his house, I walked around and found his back door unlocked. It was dark in his home, and the light switches I found didn't illuminate the underground food pantry at all. After searching for several minutes, I finally found a giant flashlight in a drawer in the kitchen. When I returned to the pantry, I found at least one hundred large mason jars full of weed on the shelf, but I didn't see any money.

This is when I thought back to some conversations I had with Billy. When I described the tunnel going to the old storm cellar, Billy was confident that this tunnel no longer existed. He said the food pantry still existed, but there was no storm cellar or tunnel anymore. I didn't think much about this at the time, but a few weeks later, he said that he had discovered a tunnel behind a shelf of canning jars that led to a bunker. This is where he found his dad's secret stash of guns. He said that must have been the storm cellar I was talking about. This led me to think that behind one of the shelves in the pantry, I could expect to find the entrance to the tunnel leading back to the old storm cellar. It only took a few minutes of moving the shelves around before I found which one was hiding the entrance to the tunnel.

I anticipated finding some money, a few guns, and maybe some more weed hidden in this bunker, but this was not what was found when I opened the door to this heavily modified room. What I saw when I looked around was a very elaborate gun room and what I estimated to be close to three hundred firearms of all sorts. I saw everything from simple handguns to giant war rifles.

After searching the room for several minutes, I found three large trash bags of unprocessed marijuana, several gallon zip lock bags full of dried mushrooms, and four shoe boxes full of cash. I had no idea how much money was in these shoe boxes, but it sure looked like a lot. I was shocked to have found such a vast fortune. Now, I needed to decide what I planned to do with it. I knew that it needed to be hidden somewhere other than in this bunker because it was likely that Billy's house would be searched or sold long before he could ever return to reclaim this fortune.

I thought about this for almost an hour while checking out the guns and making rough estimates of how much cash was in the shoe boxes. Then, I remembered that the basement floor of Erica's old house was only dirt when we were kids, and I was confident that it hadn't been modified since. If this were true, it would be the perfect place to dig a hole and hide all this loot. At this point, I was curious to know if my prediction was accurate, so I drove to Erica's old house, and as I predicted, the basement floor was exactly how I remembered it... nothing but dirt.

At this point, I returned to Billy's house and grabbed armfuls of loot to carry to my car. Once my Honda Civic was filled with as much loot as it could handle, I went out to the garage to find a shovel, and then I returned to Erica's old house to dig a hole to hide this peculiar fortune. I went straight to work thinking that I could dig out a hole big enough to hide all the loot by the end of the afternoon.

Unfortunately, after digging for six straight hours, I fully understood the challenges of this assignment, and it was daunting. The ground was so hard that I hardly created a hole big enough to hide the shoe boxes. I now estimated that digging a hole big enough to hide Billy's fortune would take all night. I continued to dig till about midnight before I finally stopped. I only got an hour of sleep the night before. My muscles were sore, and I was utterly exhausted, so I decided to go home for the night with the intention to return the following day and continue digging.

I finally finished digging the hole late in the afternoon the following day and then spent the next couple of hours filling it full of loot. Until now, nothing had weighed on my conscience, and I thought digging this hole was a noble endeavor. However, when it came time to bury the shoe boxes, I hesitated to think about the future of this cash and who would uncover it. Understanding that there was essentially no chance that Billy would be the one to uncover his fortune, I decided that I might as well take some of it with me.

It wasn't difficult to take some of this fortune of cash, but it was hard to determine how much I wanted to take. After several minutes of deep thought, I finally decided to take just one of the four shoeboxes of cash and bury the rest. I figured, if nothing else, I would eventually tell Erica about the loot to put toward her father's heart transplant. After this decision was finalized, I covered the loot with a tarp and some hay before finally covering it with dirt. By late evening, I had finished this daunting task and was so exhausted again that I had little choice but to return home and rest.

When I woke up the following morning, I felt ready to leave my hometown... possibly for good. So, I left the letter that I wrote to my folks in the mailbox and then drove over to Adam's parents' house to leave his letter in their mailbox. It was cloudy that morning. I remember it beginning to rain when I was getting ready to leave Ogallala. This weather fit my mood spot on because I was feeling dark and gloomy, just like the sky. The only thing I had going for me was that I had roughly forty-eight hours before the police would start looking for me. I figured this left me plenty of time to travel a long distance away from this hellhole before a warrant was issued for my arrest.

Before leaving town, I drove by Erica's house again, hoping to see her car, but I was not surprised when I didn't see it, so I continued down this road of disappointment to the small supermarket where Erica worked. This was my last hope to find Erica. When I pulled into the parking lot, I was surprised and excited to see Erica's car. After parking my car beside hers, I spent the next few minutes looking through the storefront window, trying to come up with the right words to say to Erica.

I noticed her in one of the aisles stocking the shelves, and she looked miserable. I had no idea what was causing her to look so sad, but this caused a deeper cut to this painful experience. I didn't think it would be possible to feel worse than I already felt, but seeing Erica's melancholy expression somehow accomplished this. This was when I noticed the coffee can with her dad's picture on it, which Erica set out to raise money for her father's heart transplant. I knew the money that I added to the can over the last couple of months was more than the rest of the town put together because I typically saw only a few coins in it before I added all the money in my wallet. I knew that this was likely not the entire reason for Erica's sad expression, but I'm sure it wasn't helping.

I thought pretty hard about this coffee can and Erica's disappointment every time she looked in the can to find only a few lousy coins. This is what led to my decision to take as much money out of my shoebox as it would take to fill that coffee can completely full of cash. I didn't want Erica or anyone else to notice me doing this, so I waited until the cashier left the front counter to help a customer before running into the store. I was able to accomplish this noble mission with just enough time to open the lid to the can and fill it full of cash without being noticed. Just as I put the lid back on, Erica looked over and saw me.

"Oliver, what are you doing here?" Erica asked, walking toward me with a surprised look on her face.

"I came to say goodbye."

"Goodbye?" she responded. "Where are you going?"

"I'm sorry, I can't tell you that right now," I said.

"What do you mean you can't tell me?" Erica asked, "Are you going to prison or something?"

"No, I just can't tell you where I am going," I replied. "Come to think of it... I don't even know where I'm going."

"What do you mean you don't know where you are going?" she asked. "You are acting strange. What's going on?"

"Listen, I really can't talk about this right now," I replied, while handing her the letter I had written. "Everything you need to know is in this envelope."

"Okay," Erica said. "I hope you are not in big trouble."

"I'm not, at least not yet, anyway. I need to get going, but I want to say one last thing to you before I go."

"What do you want to tell me?"

"I love you."

"I love you too, Oliver."

"Goodbye," I said, turning back toward the door.

"Goodbye."

This was an incredibly sad time in each of our lives. Erica didn't understand what was happening, and I had no idea when I would see her again. I just hoped that fate would bring us back together someday. After I returned to my car, I noticed Erica standing in the window looking at me. This image of contrasting beauty and sadness is something I will never forget. It wasn't just raining when the time finally arrived for me to leave my hometown... the whole fucking world was crying.

www.ingramcontent.com/pod-product-compliance
Lightning Source LLC
Chambersburg PA
CBHW021547310726
48972CB00003B/710